REMEMBER I LEFT YOU EACH OTHER

Remember I Left You Each Other

The Spring Edition

MICHAELA RYANNE

Michaela Ryanne, Steffanie Moyer

Michaela Ryanne Publishing

Remember I Left You Each Other
Michaela Ryanne

Not knowing when the dawn will come, I open every door.
-Emily Dickinson

To my father, it would have been nice to have more time with you.
To my mother, thank you for being the parent who was there for me.

<u>1</u>

Growing up, summer was my favorite season in Castine.

The heat was an excellent excuse to always be in the water. I didn't have school, so my best friend, Arlo, and I could have all the sleepovers we wanted. My brother and sister would stay with me playing games in my room. Most importantly, my dad was home.

He was a published mystery novelist who traveled often. Since his publishing office was in Vancouver, he spent a great deal of time there except in the summer. He was a stay-at-home dad every day, which my siblings and I loved. Sometimes, when I woke up in the morning, I would smell his famous blueberry waffles and espresso from my room. My little brother, Taylor, and my baby sister, Reed, would fight me over who got the last waffle, and my father would laugh while he watched all of us. My mom was busy teaching summer school, but we had barbeques, game nights, and movie nights when she got off. I remember thinking that I was not living unless it was summer. And then it would become fall...

As the leaves fell, so did the mood of my family. My dad would be busy working on his new book, so my mom would complain that she was the only one who did anything for all of us. Taylor would get busy with track and lacrosse while Reed got lost in whoever she was dating. I was usually alone with my books and thoughts when Arlo was cheerleading. There were no legendary blueberry waffles or family game nights because life, as it seemed back then, fell flat when flip-flops were no longer the shoes you grabbed to wear for the day.

I decided not to dwell on the uneasy feelings regarding my family's issues. Something I came up with was looking forward to college. New York University was my dream! I wanted to be a screenwriter, and going to the heart of talent was an excellent way to do that. I could be writing a comedy while living in the Upper East Side, drinking my expensive lattes, and not worrying that when I was sixteen, I never felt wanted by my family. I never thought I needed much, either. I could get away from all this pain and be excited about my life.

Four years ago, my dream came true. Arlo and I were accepted to NYU, so we decided to move there and be roommates. We both had to work two jobs while full-time students, but we were doing it! I had the opportunity to work on two sets but didn't get to write on either. All I did was get coffee and lunch, but the people I was getting those things for were some of the best in the business, and when the time came around to hire me, they would remember me. Arlo did a fantastic job dancing in almost every school show and had a giant following on social media, which is helpful when we need groceries for the week. We have expensive lattes in the morning together before school, which is extraordinary. In four months, our college lives are over, and our post-grad lives begin. Hopefully, I will have a job by then.

Everything seemed to be going according to plan until tonight when my phone rang, and Taylor's name appeared on my phone. I don't have to answer it to know that something was wrong. My stomach gets tight, and I begin to feel nauseous. Taylor has early classes in Maine, so he wouldn't be calling me right now if it wasn't necessary. I hit the green button on my phone and hold my breath, "Taylor, what's wrong?"

"Maggie, Dad had a heart attack." I hear his voice trying not to cry into the phone. "He... didn't make it."

I shake my head like he is wrong, but I know he isn't. He wouldn't call me if there was a possibility that he was wrong. "What are you talking about?"

"Mags, they took him into the ICU a little while ago, but they couldn't help him. He... he just died."

He just died. It didn't sound right. He wouldn't just die on everyone.

Except he did die.

My father died and I have not spoken to him in a year.

2

Arlo and I took a flight out this morning in order to get to the funeral on time. We won't have any time to change before we get to the cemetery so we had to be dressed on the plane. Eyes lingered on us the whole flight as if we worked for death himself and they were spooked.

Taylor and I spent hours on the phone in the middle of the night last night talking about Mom, Dad, Grandma, and the town. My family lives in Castine, Maine which has a population of approximately 1,400 people. It was right by the water and the subject of my father's first crime novel, In The Dead of Night. It was about a series of murders involving stay-at-home women (my mom tried hard to not read into it) who were murdered over the span of ten years. It was a masterpiece and after news hit of my father's passing, it was at the top of the New York Times best-seller list.

I was not thrilled to go back to my childhood home in that town where everyone thought my family was perfect. Sometimes I wondered what life would be like if I broke all of their hearts and told them what it was like in that house when no one was around, but I didn't have it in me.

"Hey," Arlo says, grabbing my hand, "It's going to be okay; you know that don't you?"

I laughed a little, "The only thing that I know is that I am going to have to spend the next week back home listening to everyone say my father was a great man." Otis Honors was at best an okay man and an average father. The only thing remarkable about him was his writing and considering that was all he cared about, I would say he got exactly what he wanted out of his life while he was here.

"He wasn't great," Arlo adds, "but he was your father and despite how you are acting right now, I know you're grieving." Our grip gets tighter, "It's okay to love someone even when they weren't what you wanted them to be."

I didn't disagree with her. There was no use when she was right- I did love him. I didn't like him and as far as I know, he didn't like me, but I have spent the last few years of my life distancing myself from Castine and everyone in it. It didn't occur to me they wouldn't always be there when I was ready to go back. We spend the rest of the flight in silence dreading the eventual arrival into the small town we haven't been back to since we left for college.

My mother sent a car.

When I spoke to Taylor last night, he said mother was thrilled to see me even under the circumstances and she would pick me up herself. We looked around for five minutes before Arlo finally saw the sign that said Cunningham and Honors. I had to give it to my mother; she knew how to be a classy bitch, but a bitch nonetheless.

The ride there was all too familiar. We passed by Bridgeport Mall which was the closest thing we had to a shopping center near Castine. The Regal Theater was still standing next to the church off of Newvalley Drive. Most importantly, the waterfront cafe. It was a small cafe by the coast where everyone went to get coffee in the morning. I went there because Arlo's brother, Ashton, was a server. He also happened to be the love of my life not that he was aware of that fact. I would go there after school when Arlo had practice and do my homework while listening to Billy Joel. Occasionally when Ashton didn't have any customers, he would come over and take one of my headphones and listen to him with me. I missed those days a great deal. He was probably one of the only people besides Taylor and Reed that I missed.

I missed them like crazy, but I was still nervous to see them. When I left for college Taylor took it the hardest. We were siblings, but he was also my friend. I went to all of his games and he read all of my award-winning essays. We were only thirteen months apart so when it came to having stuff in common we were linked to the hip. All of my favorite songs were his songs. Our favorite TV shows and movies were the same. When I told him I was leaving, he was distraught and didn't speak to me for several days. The only reason he did was that Reed, aka the family shrink, told him they could visit me in New York and have the best sibling vacations. Every year they come to see me for spring break, except for this year. This time I was coming to visit them.

The driver let us out deep into the cemetery at the bottom of the hill where my father's funeral was taking place. "I'm dropping the rest of your things off at your house with the housekeeper as your mother instructed." Arlo thanked him with a tip and before he drove off he added, "I am sorry for your loss."

The words go to my throat like a scarf being used to choke someone. It takes me more than a minute to catch my breath but when I do I know this isn't the last time I will be hearing those words from people that know nothing about me today.

The priest is already speaking when Arlo and I join the funeral party so we try to be quiet. That plan fails because Reed runs over to me screaming with joy and asks us to catch her. "Maggie!" She says wrapping her arms around me, "Thank God you're here! This shit is boring."

Reed is just being Reed so Mother doesn't seem offended, just annoyed. I ignore her and reach for Reed's hand pulling her behind me so we can get in line. The priest continues his sermon keeping a watchful eye on me. It takes me a moment to recognize him but it's Pull-Out Pollen. A memory of Arlo telling me he was in and out in less than a minute makes me crack a smile. I nudge Taylor and ask, "Why is Pull-Out our priest?"

He shrugs and says, "Push-In was unavailable."

"Would you two knock it off!" My mother hisses at us. I have to hide behind Taylor's shoulders to hide my laughter.

"It is never an easy thing to say goodbye to someone who made an impact on this earth, but the pain will ease knowing they are going to a better place," Pollen attempts to continue, but Reed doesn't let him.

"Where exactly is he going? He was an atheist." She whispers to us.

"Not in this town he wasn't," Taylor adds.

Castine is and has always been a small town where people go to church every Sunday. It didn't matter what kind, just as long as you went. My father didn't believe in organized religions; however, when someone would ask he would say a different one each time. It was sort of a game to see what he went with as his answer. I remember he once said astrology and people were horrified.

"Maybe with his secret family," I say.

"Or maybe to that island that Tupac is on," Reed said giggling.

"He is definitely having drinks with Princess Diana somewhere," Taylor whispered.

My mother smacks us all on the back of the head and then leans in to whisper, "Shut it now!"

Ah, I think to myself, I feel like I never left.

3

Once the funeral was over, my mother got me and my siblings into the limo she hired for the day and everyone packed into their own cars traveling behind us to our house.

Our house was a stunning ocean-front cottage. It was two stories with a black deck around it and rose bushes surrounding the trim. I remember thinking that it was strange they never redecorated the front because it was so old, but my Mom loved the style of it since the day she and Dad moved in. Once she made up her mind, it was the final call, and I guess in that way, we are alike.

When I moved away for college, I saw it as an escape from the place that I felt made me hold my breath. My mom was always upset with me for something and my dad, when he was there, wasn't invested in my life like he was when I was little. Taylor and I were close, but he had his friends and the occasional significant other. Reed was just her own chaotic self. If she had a girlfriend, then she was even more chaotic and wild. I had Arlo and Ashton and my babysitting job was by all means a mistake of its own. Life seemed to be moving too fast for me to keep up or too still for it to seem significant.

Now that I am 22 and facing the thing I ran away from, it doesn't look the same. It's the same house on the same street with the same nosey neighbors, but it doesn't look like that place I used to avoid after school. Even Mom, who usually has to insert her opinion into everything, seems far too quiet.

As we walked into the house, Mya, our housekeeper, greeted us with the smell of delicious food like red velvet cookies and mint chocolate cookies. They are the staple desserts that she usually made when someone needed cheering up. I want to go eat something, but Taylor gives me a stack of plates and tells me to set the table. The last time I was here, we still had our old oakwood table my grandfather handmade for Mom and Dad when they first bought this house, but this new one is modern wood with harsh lines and no character. Setting the plates down, I notice the rug is new too. The paintings my mom made when she was a teenager and Reed's from high school are no longer displayed, instead, there are white canvases with gold detailing. I am sure if I looked all over this house many things would be different. I just didn't understand why everything impersonal was in the place of something that meant a great deal to our family, I didn't understand why it looked like a celebrity giving a tour to Architectural Digest.

"Reed," she stops herself from leaving the dining room and looks to me inquisitively, "What happened to the table and mom's painting?"

She rolls her eyes, "She is having a photographer from a magazine come show the house next week. She wanted it to look updated for that. Everything is in storage."

I am not even surprised, "Of course she did," I mutter to myself.

"Just be nice today. Our dad died, but he was also her husband." My sweet Reed. She is always trying to keep the peace.

I nod my head and she takes that as an agreement. In my heart, I am broken. He was my father and I loved him. In my head, I find it laughable that they were still married knowing how they made each other miserable, but in a town this small and with his family man reputation in the book world, I knew they wouldn't divorce. Maybe if they had then they could still be friends who did their best to raise their kids. Perhaps I wouldn't feel so down in my childhood home. Maybe we would feel like a normal family.

The sound of everyone shuffling through the front door catches my attention but instead of running to greet everyone, I have to run away. My heart feels so heavy with all of the changes in the house and the fact that my father isn't in his study like he usually would be on a weekend when he is home so I decide that hiding is my best option. Running down the hall to his study, I slide the doors apart and shut myself in. *Breathe...* I think to myself. *All you need to do is breathe and play the good daughter just like you planned.*

"Hey you," a familiar voice startles me and sends shivers down my spine. I turn around and see Jamie. My old boss as well as my old fling. My old mistake wrapped up in a cunning yet sexy persona that is currently standing in my safe place.

"Why are you here?"

He puts down the picture of me with my father at the national spelling bee I won when I was four. "It's a funeral and I am a close friend of your family." I know why he's here and it has nothing to do with paying respects to my father and everything to do with messing with my head when I am vulnerable. It used to be his favorite game until I pulled out of playing to go to college.

"I mean why are you in my father's office?"

"Your mom asked me to make sure there were some nice photos spread out in the house for when the guests got here. By the sound of the baseless sympathies and your heels hitting the hardwood floor as you ran in here; I am guessing people are here."

"They are and you should go join them. I am sure Leo is waiting for you." Leo is his stunning wife and the mother of his children. They are all blue-eyed and perfect. I was so used to watching his kids every day I used to be able to tell them apart but I doubt I would be able to now. They probably look too similar.

"She's out of town with the kids. My mother-in-law was having some unfortunate heart problems so she'll see Val when she gets back."

He makes having a sick relative sound like an opportunity instead of a hardship. It surprises me how similar he looks from when I saw him last. His broad frame and dark features are the same but his beard is new. He looks almost 30 now, but not in the wrong way more like it suits him being older. It always has.

"Jamie, I need a minute alone."

He swiftly walks by me but before he goes whispers, "Always good to see you Mags."

Oh yeah... Coming back home is sure to be the death of me.

<u>4</u>

Jamie is here without his wife or kids, Ashton is soon to arrive, and Arlo is going to kill me if she thinks for even a moment I let myself be alone with the same man she has wanted to murder for years.

I decided to make my way to the living room to greet everyone with my family instead of sulking in the study. Everyone from town must be here because there is barely enough room for me to stand once I get into the mourning room. My mother is crowded by all of her girlfriends, Taylor is surrounded by his frat bros, and Reed is standing teary-eyed by our evil grandmother Jackie. My mother is something else but my Grandmother Jackie is something unknown to everyone. I give it an hour before she criticizes my mother for the choice of her hairstyle for the funeral.

The funny thing is that as people walk by me and offer their condolences, I seem to be the only person out of my entire family they don't bother fibbing to. The others get sappy stories and half-truths about what a great man my father was despite not really being present in this town for most of the year, but no one bothers with me. I think they know I don't care who they thought my dad was because they didn't know him and I didn't either. I couldn't tell you if he had any allergies or what his favorite movie was. I am fairly certain I couldn't tell them his birthday off the top of my head (Reed always reminds me) because he was a stranger to me. I wish I didn't feel so out of place here.

"You look like you could use some fresh air," I smile because I know who's speaking to me before I turn around- Ashton.

When I look at him, there's this weight that lifts off of my shoulders and I don't hesitate before I give him my hand. "Please," I beg him.

He leads me out the back door and even though I know Jamie is looking I don't care. Ashton Channing is here and everything is going to be okay.

It's cooler outside so Ashton gives me his jacket. As he places it on my shoulders, he moves my hair out of the way and those butterflies I used to get from him when I was younger start up again. He doesn't say anything for a moment so I decide to, "Are you not going to ask me how I'm doing?" There's some sarcasm in my voice and he hears it.

"Come on Mags," he says casually, "I know you better than to do that."

We take a seat on the patio, even though the air is still colder than we would like to sit comfortably outside. Ashton is one of those people whose presence is calming and nothing needs to be said between us in order for me to be grateful he is here.

"It's only been two weeks since your birthday," he says like it's supposed to hurt worse when you just turned 22 and then your Dad dies.

"Do you know what he got me for my birthday this year?" Ashton shakes his head no, "He sent me a copy of his book and the keys to my new car in the garage here."

I remember opening up the box he and Mom sent me. Inside were keys to a Toyota Prius which I won't use because I live in New York and don't drive and then a copy of his own book. I thought that maybe there was a dedication to me but instead found a quote, "Don't ever think that just because you do things differently, you're wrong." It is from Gail Tsukiyama. I still don't know what he was referring to.

"I think your dad's main problem was that no matter what he did, he couldn't do the one thing required of a parent."

"What would that be?"

"Be there for you."

A sharp pain hits my stomach causing me to grip it intensely. "Well, it's too late to worry about that now." I mean it. What good is it to be mad at a ghost?

"You can do that with whoever else you want to, but not me, Maggie." His tone is serious and so sharp it almost feels like it could cut me.

"Do what, Ashton?"

"That thing where you pretend you don't have feelings because you think you are not allowed to have them."

I hold his gaze where his deep chocolate brown eyes are on mine worrying he can see right through me and that he always has. Taking a deep breath I say, "Why don't you go find your girlfriend in there instead of trying to be my therapist?"

As I walk away I hear him say something about his girlfriend but I don't want to know anything about her. I know she's dating him and she lives here and both of those things are going to drive me to insanity so I leave in pursuit of Arlo.

I find her getting her palm read by Reed in my room. The two of them have kindred spirits since they are both so hopeful and sensitive to other people's problems. Reed loves to be there for people, especially when they don't ask, and since she can't do that with me her nosey little self has set sights on Arlo. If I had to guess it would be something involving the frat boy Fez she's been seeing casually.

"So," Reed says, gliding her fingers along the lines of Arlo's palm, "I see your fate line has moved since the last time I saw you."

"What does that mean?" Arlo asked, wrinkling her brow with concern.

"It means there's a shift in your life coming. Have you felt a major change?"

Arlo grins mischievously, "Maybe I have."

"I think I might vomit." I interrupt.

Reed ignores me and continues. I take a seat next to her as she reads Arlo's palm taking into account that while I don't believe in this, I think it's essential to let Reed.

"I would bet that someone you are hoping to get closer to is not too far from your grasp." Damnit. I mutter to myself. It's the stupid frat boy.

A knock at the door gets all of our attention, "You all need to get downstairs," Mother says. It's not a request, it's a demand and we do so because it will be worse if we don't listen.

My father is dead. Today is all about the fact that he's gone and for the next week I'm in this house with my family wondering what today would've felt like if I had called him before he died.

<u>5</u>

Funerals have freaked me out since I was a little girl.

It was the thought that when someone died we all sat around and glorified a person that was flawed. My father was the perfect example of someone I did not think deserved that treatment.

The halls of this house paint a different picture today. While some of the furniture has been replaced and new decor hangs on the walls, so do family portraits. My mother has gotten all the photos with my dad and my siblings and plastered every free space with them in the living room. It is like some freaky exhibit in memoriam of Otis Kingsley Honors. My eyes stay glued to a picture of me and him at my spelling bee contest when I was ten. I spent two weeks reminding him and my mom it was an important event and I wanted them both to be there, only to get on the stage and see only Taylor sitting amongst the crowd. I was so angry that I wanted to win the trophy just to show them what they missed. Each time it was my turn, my head went over the booklet that was given to each of us the month prior and I read each letter out until I made it to the final round. My dad ran in, sweaty and out of breath. Once I saw him sit down next to Taylor and wave at me from his seat, all of the anger left me as did my need to win and I lost. I still got runner-up but I didn't care because my dad promised that he'd be there and he was. My eyes start to get watery when I realize that was the last time that he showed up for me.

"Maggie dear?" Mrs. Sutten asks me.

"I'm sorry," I say, snapping back to reality, "What were you saying?"

"I was just asking if you have a boyfriend at school?"

The thing is that I don't have a boyfriend. I have spent years at college and only dated one person. Their name was Blue and while they were lovely they didn't love me. I am too emotionally unavailable and unwilling to partake in being needy. I do not wish to share this information as I am already enough of a basket case in this town. "Oh, yeah, his name is Henry. He is a marketing major."

"That is lovely! He'll be able to take good care of you when he graduates."

I literally want to punch this sexist old lady, but I just laugh and say, "Here's hoping."

From across the room, I see Taylor talking to Father Pull Out and Reed with Mother and Nanna. None of us seem pleased by our current situation. I hate funerals.

It's nine P.M. when everyone finally leaves the house. I assist in helping Taylor clean up while Reed and Mom stand at the door thanking everyone for coming. Arlo and Ashton left an hour ago but she will be here first thing in the morning to worry about me some more.

We are working in the kitchen in silence when Mother comes in and sounds exhausted, "Well, everyone is finally gone including that God-awful woman Sharon!"

"Um, mom," Reed interrupts, "That is our grandmother."

"I know who she is." She kisses us each on the cheek and leaves us for the night.

"You have to give it to her," Taylor says, "She's an honest woman."

Reed laughs a little, "Grandmomma is a racist hag so I will give it to her this time."

"Why don't you guys take showers and head to bed, I will finish the kitchen."

"Are you sure?" Taylor asks.

"Yeah, it's been a long day, so I will take kitchen duty."

They both hug me and head up to bed, leaving me by myself. My yellow gloves were immersed under the water as I scrubbed the dishes clean. It is a nice moment since I have not been by myself all day. Through the kitchen window, I can see snow begin to fall. The soft white setting brings me some sense of peace after the day I have had. It's been a mixture of emotions from sadness to contentment. Parents die. It is a reality of life, but what do you do when you aren't sure who you are mourning?

After finishing the dishes, I begin to pick up the other areas of the house starting with my father's study. When I slide the doors open, I feel instantly irritated that people were in here today. The other places in the house don't feel like people were violating the space, but here, where my father was his truest self, feels as though they were disrespecting it altogether.

I put the trash bag on the floor and sat at his desk. It is the same cherry oak wooden desk from when I was a little girl. We moved in here like one big happy family and the second that Reed came along it felt like my father had no time for me; however, there were some nights when I couldn't sleep, so I came down here. I knew he would be working late on his book because it was the only time he had time to write since he worked all day at school teaching English. Instead of sending me back to bed, he would tell me to join him.

"Babes," he'd call me, "Come sit on my desk and I'll read you some of my book." I would hop into his arms so he could rest me on top of his desk. I remember him pulling open his drawer to get out his outline and flipping open the false bottom, "Remember sweetheart, if you ever need to hide something of value put it in here. I won't even question it if it is some candy and you don't want me to tell Mommy."

For fun, I pull the drawer open and undo the latch that re-leases the false bottom. My heart stops when I see some stuff is actually inside. I see three large stacks of envelopes each labeled with a different name Maggie, Taylor, and Reed. Grabbing my stack I notice a small sticky note that the others don't have. *Read your letters first Maggie.* My letters? What the hell is going on here?

Each envelope is numbered so I pull on number one and rip it open.

February 22, 2000

Dear Maggie,

Today is now my favorite day. You are currently fast asleep in your bassinet next to your equally exhausted mother. We spent over twelve hours just waiting for you to be born and an hour of your mother actually giving birth. It's a rollercoaster of emotions though, because I have never been this tired but excited at the same time. I keep looking over at you and memorizing everything about you. They told us some-times babies come out looking different than you'd expect but you're stunning just like your mother. You've got her soft cheeks, dark eyes, dark eyebrows, and adorable nose. I know that once you get older you are going to look a little more like me or at least act a little more like me, but for now, I think you are perfect.

I was eighteen when I fell in love with your mother and for some reason, she fell in love with me too. She is more stunning, comes from a better family, and is all in all a much better person than I am and she chose me to be with. I thought life couldn't get better than that until I came home from college one day and your mother told me she was pregnant. It was like I had all of the coffee in the world. I was so excited.

Today marks the beginning of your life and the beginning of my life as well. You have given me something that I never expected. You made me into a father, my love.

Love, Dad.

<u>6</u>

My fingers trace over the words as if this letter was some kind of historical artifact. The paper feels so old and yet hasn't been wrinkled over time due to staying in the protective case of the envelope. All these letters have been saved waiting for the perfect moment to make themselves known to me and the others. Oh God... Taylor and Reed have letters too. He's going to shock them like this too.

Grabbing the stack, I count all the way up to 22. Every year, even this year, over two weeks ago, my father wrote a letter addressed to me on my birthday. They went past far when I assumed he stopped caring about being a father, especially a father to me.

"You made me into a father, my love." The words bang around in my head giving me a headache. There's something about how he calls me "my love" that sounds vaguely familiar but not something I can place. It scares me that I feel as though I don't know him. I don't know this version of him. He sounds so in love with my mom and in love with being a father. What happened to him?

A sudden bang from upstairs startles me so I shove the letters back into the drawer and close the false bottom. I ran upstairs so fast I surely woke up the entire household but fear overtakes me so I do not care. Once my door shuts, I take off my clothes from the day and change outfits. My soft sweater pajama set is comforting and rubs against my skin softly as I pace back and forth in my room.

This is what I know. I know that my father wrote each of his kid's letters for every single one of our birthdays. I know that the letters will most likely reveal why over the years he became distant. What I don't know is why he left them for me to find. Nobody knew about the false bottom in the drawer but me and even a note told me to read mine first, but why me? Out of all of us, I am the worst daughter. I haven't been home in ages and I didn't speak to him for the last year. I am also the one who started most arguments when it came to him and me. None of this is adding up to him leaving me something so personal.

My phone goes off and I jump for it immediately. A text from Ashton appears.

Unlock your window.

I walk over to my window and unlock it, seeing a tall Ashton waiting to be let in as he clings to the cold pipe on the side of my house. "What are you doing here?" I hiss at him as he climbs into my bedroom.

"I, oh fuck," he yelps as his foot gets caught on my window sill and his foot breaks through the glass. My hands go to my temples to restrain myself from pushing him back out the damn window. "I will fix that!" He assures me.

"Other than trying to kill me via pneumonia; why are you here?"

He stumbles to his feet and groans, "I don't have a girlfriend."

"Uh, okay then thanks for stopping by in the middle of the night for that breaking news segment."

"I wanted to say that earlier when you mentioned it, but I didn't, and it has been bothering me all day."

My head is spinning. There is far too much happening today. "This isn't something that could have waited until tomorrow?"

He shakes his head no, "Like I said, it was bothering me."

My stomach starts to feel sick so I sit on the edge of my bed and Ashton follows me. I thought I knew what was going to happen today. I wasn't expecting to go to my father's funeral, see my neighbor who I had an affair with, talk to the love of my life about said father, and find letters from my dead father all in one day. It's funny to think that I thought my mother was going to be the biggest problem I was going to deal with.

"I'm so exhausted."

His arm wraps up around my waist, "Get in bed. I'll stay for a little and then wait for you to fall asleep."

I agree and let him help me into bed. The peace I feel with him in the room helps keep my head attached to my neck. After he turns off the lights, he climbs into bed with me and the two of us are silent as we drift off to sleep unaware that this is the first time he's ever slept alone with me since we were kids having a sleepover.

"Good morning!" The shrill sound of my mother's voice echoes throughout my room waking Ashton and me up. She sits at the end of my bed smiling at us as if she is enjoying the embarrassment she's causing.

"Morning Mrs. Honors," Ashton says, running his fingers through his hair, "I didn't mean to fall asleep here."

"Well, considering you're both fully dressed, it is none of my concern. But I am going to ask about the window being broken," she says pointing to my windowsill where the pieces of glass are still scattered.

I laugh a little, "I was trying to run away again."

She nods her head like she's pretending to care and begins to walk out, but before she leaves she stops at my door and says, "Ashton, you are always welcome here. Besides, at least she has a boyfriend now."

Once she is gone I reach for my remote to throw at her, but Ashton stops me, 'No, no, no!"

<u>7</u>

All I want to do is read another one of my letters, but instead, I am subjected to breakfast with my family. It is torture honestly. I have my mother who will not stop and listen to me when I say Ashton is not my boyfriend, my best friend who thinks I slept with her brother and my brother who thinks I slept with his best friend. The only normal person is Reed and the irony in that is not lost on me.

When I get downstairs, everyone turns to look at me with such surprise I worry they think I have never had a guy in my room before. I am 22 and filled with commitment issues so of course I have had a few guys in my room. "Morning," I mutter while pouring myself some coffee.

"Sweetheart," Mother says, "Is Ashton going to be escorting you to the stars ball at the cafe tonight?"

"We're going to that? We had Dad's funeral yesterday!" Keeping up with appearances is my mother's favorite pastime.

"Of course we are! Daddy would have wanted to go." Reed adds.

"Please!" Taylor says, "He wasn't home during this time of the year to go."

Come to think of it, why was he home? When I got the call from Taylor that dad had passed, he said mom found him in their bedroom. The thing is, that this time of the year he was in New York or Seattle with his publishers, especially when one of his books was turning into a movie. Why was he home in Castine when he was so busy?

"I... I don't have anything to wear for that mom."

"Don't worry darling, you have plenty of time to go shopping with Arlo before tonight. She said she doesn't have anything either."

I rolled my eyes at her, "Well, I got a text message from her less than ten minutes ago that said 'Thanks for jumping my brother and not telling me you bitch.'" Taylor laughed, choking on his biscuit, "So I am not sure if she wants to go shopping right now."

"Just tell her nothing happened! Everyone knew you had a thing for him anyway. I doubt she was the only one who didn't."

"Thank you for that!" I yell at her.

"Mags, I'm going tonight with Reed. Go with us! The Honors trio is back!"

I smile a little to myself. It's been such a long time since we have called each other that. It's more common in this town to have a family here but most people have a maximum of two or four kids. Since we were the only one that had three they called us the Honors Trio. There was one Halloween we had T-shirts made. "Okay," I say, "Let's go. Let me just straighten things out with Arlo."

"Good luck with that," Taylor tells me. I know I need it.

When we were younger and Arlo had free time, she would usually be at the gym doing laps in the pool. Arlo is the athletic one with her dancing, swimming, and ice skating talents. I tell her she would be an excellent candidate for the bachelor and she doesn't believe me.

I see her from the edge of the pool slicing through the water like a hot knife through butter. Her bright red hair is slicked back in a swimmer's cap so she can move easily. "Arlo!" I yell for her.

She stops and takes a look back at me. I can tell just from her scrunched-up face and furrowed brows she is not happy. Imagine if she knew I actually was in love with him? She might kill me. "What's up brother fucker?"

I rolled my eyes at her, "Nothing happened! My mother is a gossip, you know that!"

"I know!" she yells at me from across the pool, "I just don't like the thought of the two in bed together!"

I stomp my foot on the concrete, frustrated with her lack of reasoning, "Would you get out of the damn pool?"

She abides by my request and hops out of the pool. She leads me to the bleachers where I sit down and I feel her fury heating her from the inside out. Taking off her swimmer's cap she says, "I have always known you liked him. I just never thought anything would happen with the two of you, especially because Jamie fucked you up so badly."

"Arlo, nothing happened," I assure her, reaching for her hand.

"I am okay with it if something does, just please tell me."

I am taken aback by her permission to pursue something Ashton. Ever since we were kids, Arlo hated it when I paid even the slightest bit of my attention to him. Their parents had a tendency to do that, and I knew it would break her heart if I did. "I think I just need to focus on myself right now. No boys or creepy older men need to be on my radar."

"His wife and kids are out of town. Did he tell you that?"

Jamie is someone who no one knew about except for me and Arlo. With everything going on, it is going to be almost impossible for me to see him and that is something I take pleasure in knowing. "I'm not going to see him anymore. It was wrong of us to do that in the first place."

"It was wrong of him to take advantage of a depressed young woman he could manipulate into thinking they were dating. I know you blame yourself a lot, but he was an adult. He should have left you alone."

I think the logical part of me always wanted to think of it that way. If I could blame him and move on, everything would be better, and I would feel better, but that is not true. I know it was not the reality of my situation back then. "Obviously if I could go back in time and not do it I would. I just do not want to engage with him while I am here. Plus, I have some more pressing issues at the moment." I pull out the first letter from my father out of my purse and give it to her.

As her eyes began to glide over the letter, I felt less alone. I couldn't tell everyone what this was because I still didn't understand where these letters might take me, but I knew with Arlo everything would eventually feel okay again.

8

"Why have you never seen these letters before? Why would he wait now?" Arlo asked me as we tried on some gowns in the dressing room of Moonlight Boutique.

If I was going to the dance tonight with Taylor and Reed, I would have to look stunning. They are both impeccable at dressing themselves. If I go for a coffee run, then I don't usually dress in dress pants and silk blouses like Reed does or soft white button-ups that look like they are from a period piece like Taylor. The Honors trio is back and we need to look like it.

"For the millionth time, I have no idea why! I haven't even read the other letters yet. I was so freaked out by that one."

I am not being entirely honest. The problem with these letters is that if I keep reading, then I could get all of the answers to my questions. He could be honest with me for once in his life and that might kill me. Knowing everything that happened could possibly be the death of me.

"It's just creepy! I truly need all of the details!"

I groan, "I will make you a cliff note."

Every dress I look at on these racks doesn't have the certain flare I am looking for. I need stunning, not dull. It's our first family outing since Dad died, so people will be expecting to see us in mourning, and my mother won't accept anything less than fabulous.

"Here me out," Arlo says, "How about this one?" She holds up a pale pink satin gown with little stars stitched into it along the hips and hem of the dress. It's the definition of stunning.

"I think that it's perfect," I say, grabbing it. "Now, let's get out of here! I have to go home and get ready, and by me, I mean you."

When I got back home, no one was there. It's the perfect time to go into the study and read another letter.

February 1, 2001

Dear Maggie,

I used to think that loving someone was something that happened over time. You see a girl from across the room. Your heart starts to beat too fast by just the sheer thought of getting to know them. By the time they speak their first word to you, you know that you will fall in love with them because life is just like that. It's all about timing and falling in love with people that begin to mean everything to you.

You, my love, are something that is unknown to me. I don't have to know you to understand you are the love of my life. I don't question why you laugh when you see someone riding a bike fall down on our walks (although I am praying you are not a serial killer). I don't have to know why you will only let me put you down for naps and not your mother. I still do not understand why it is when you're in the bathtub you get scared if you have a rubber ducky in the water. None of that matters because I don't have to know anything to know you mean everything to me.

Today is one of those days as a parent that I am eternally grateful for my life because not only are you one year old but you are going to have a baby brother soon! You're so happy about it that for your birthday you asked that people bring gifts for you to play with your little brother (well your version of telling me that. Stringing sentences together is not your strong suit.) You are all about sharing and I adore that.

I am going to make today perfect for you because today is my favorite day since you made me a father.

All my love,

Dad

Is my birthday his favorite day or was it his favorite day?

He adored something about me.

He loved everything about me even if he didn't understand me yet.

This person, whoever he was, went missing quite some time ago, and meeting him would have been magical. Just reading how he used to feel about me made me feel better about myself because I was the love of his life back then. Before all the noise of being a busy author and a husband, I meant absolutely everything to him.

I didn't realize that tears formed in my eyes until they fell down onto the letter. The paper is so old and I don't want to ruin it so I fold it back up and shove it into the envelope labeled 2.

As I shove the drawer close, Mother appears in the doorway knocking softly, "Maggie," she says, "Is everything okay sweetheart?"

I don't even think about it. I just asked her, "Did dad ever call me 'love' or anything?" My tears are still falling but I ignore them.

My mother grabs a cloth from her coat pocket and wipes away my tears. She takes a seat on the desk next to me. Lifting my chin up so that she is looking down at me she says, "He used to call me that. He always called me his 'love' when we were younger and he'd write me love letters. "My love, the weather affects my mood without you here with me". Cheesy stuff like that. When I got pregnant he used to point," she says pointing to her stomach, "and he'd say 'good morning my love', "I can't wait to meet you, my love'. Why do you ask?"

I pulled away from her, "I just remembered something, and I couldn't place it. I think he used to call me that."

"Until Taylor," she says.

"What do you mean?"

"Anytime we were having another baby, he would call you guys that. After Reed was born and she said she didn't like him calling her 'princess' or anything close to that, he said he would call her..."

"Lovey," I interrupted her, "He called her lovey."

That's it! That is why 'my love' sounded so damn familiar. It was me, and then Taylor, and then Reed was always 'lovey'. Even in the later years, 'lovey' was how he'd address her.

"How about you start to get ready? The dance is in a couple of hours."

"Yeah, I'll go do that." I left her in the study. I have so many more questions and in time, she might give me some more answers.

9

"I still think this is weird that we are going to a dance when Dad's funeral was just yesterday," I say as Reed helps steam out some of the wrinkles in my dress. Arlo was right, I look amazing in this.

"Am I crazy, Reed, or does that sound like the first time Maggie has actually shown some emotion since our father died."

Asshole, I think to myself, and continue to adjust my straps.

"You are not crazy," Reed says by my feet, "I am so glad! You sound so depressed!"

"What is wrong with you?" I ask looking down at her. She's dressed in a black sequined suit and black shirt. Her light brown hair is slicked back into a bun which makes the glitter hairspray she put in it look even more radiant.

She finishes steaming out the hemline of my dress and puts the steamer away in my closet. Taylor is trying on yet another blazer because to him there seems to be a huge difference between navy blue and midnight blue. Reed wanted all of us to get ready together like we used to do when we were kids, and for the most part, I think it is a cute idea, except for when they are tag-teaming me on being an emotionless freak.

"Oh Mags," Taylor says, "We love you! We just want you to feel free to share how you actually feel with us."

"Well, I feel like you guys suck."

"That's a start!" Reed yelps as she jumps up and down.

My phone goes off and a message appears from JC. *Shit!* Jamie is starting to send secret messages again. I try to grab my phone but Reed gets to it before I do.

"Ohhhhhhh," she says mischievously, "Does someone have a secret boyfriend?"

My chest starts to feel so heavy making it harder for me to breathe. I cannot tell either of them what Jamie was to me back then. Taylor would want to kill him and Reed... Reed would gladly help in burying the body. They are my younger siblings but that doesn't mean they are not protective. They are in fact overprotective.

The thing that I notice that helps me calm down is Taylor. He's so calm and not asking questions. Does he think that it's Ashton? Does he not care? He sits on my bed and sighs. Adjusting his cuffs he says, "Reed, can you ask mom if she's almost ready? We should leave soon."

"I am guessing that is a code for 'my baby sister needs to get out of the room', which may I add, is so rude!" She stomps her feet on the floor like she's a toddler throwing a tantrum and leaves my room.

The second the door closes, there's a shift in the air between us. It is much harsher than it was mere moments ago.

"So," he says, stepping a few feet closer to me. "You have a boyfriend?"

"No," I answered quickly. I'm not lying. I do not have a boyfriend. Jamie is... God, I don't even know what Jamie is. He can't be an ex-boyfriend. He's married and I was sixteen at the time. It's far too complicated to explain to my brother. "Just some guy I used to talk to."

"Are you talking to him right now?" He seemed angry, but for the life of me, I don't know why. He didn't seem mad about me possibly sleeping with Ashton.

"No, I'm not."

"Good," he goes to my door swinging it open, and finds Reed leaning against it in the hopes she might hear something. Before he heads down the hall I hear him muttering to himself, "Keep it that way."

10

I was sixteen when Jamie Cartright and his wife Leo moved in just a few houses down from my own.

When you are that young, everything feels so intense and heavy that you almost feel like it will crush you. That is precisely how it felt for me to live in this house at that time. I wasn't pretty. I wasn't skinny. I wasn't interesting enough to be with someone. I wasn't anything in comparison with other people like Arlo or Reed. My characteristics didn't shine like theirs did.

And then there was Jamie.

I was riding my bike one day after school and saw my dad and him outside our house with their beers in one hand and their bean bags in the other eagerly wanting to score a new high record. My dad invited them over to welcome them to the neighborhood (ironic considering he was the least present citizen) and to introduce them to his kids.

The second he extended his hand to mine and reached for it a little too eagerly, I felt that spark. There was an interest between us and I had no idea that we would become something secretive, passionate, and painful.

The first night we were alone, I felt like I was thrown into a delicious trap and had only myself to blame.

Leo went to visit her parents with their kids Drea and Sutten and Jamie stayed behind because he had to work the next day. He told me since the kids were gone, he wanted some help setting up their playroom for when they got back. It was a reasonable task and Mother thought I was being so lovely spending my Friday night with my neighbor. It was all so innocent–until it wasn't.

When I got to his house, he was dressed up in his Italian suit that he still had on from work but his shirt was slightly unbuttoned.

"Mags," he said breathlessly, "thank goodness you're here! I swear I'm just horrible trying to decipher instructions when Leo isn't here."

There was this way he said my name, almost like an invitation for trouble that confused me. He never talked to me like that when we were in front of other people, just when we were alone.

"Give that to me," I snatched the instructions from his hand playfully. "You're a lost cause." I dropped my bag and took off my shoes, leaving them at the door. We began to walk upstairs slowly and I felt him looking at me, knowing being here was trouble. I was asking for something that I didn't fully comprehend which was entirely different from what I assumed. For me, it was a crush. Crushes are normal and adults usually do the "I'm flattered" thing and move on, but Jamie doesn't. He knew how I felt about him. He knew I felt alone. He knew making himself available to me was an offer that at the time I couldn't refuse. He also knew that being alone with him and being offered what I thought I wanted would be exciting at the time.

When we got to the playroom the floor was bare except for plastic sheets and parts of a table and chair set that were spread out.

"So," he said, getting on his knees. "I think the best thing to start with would be the chairs since there are fewer pieces."

"Yeah probably. I'll start."

I go to grab a screwdriver and parts A and C of the parts of the wood that are labeled with this little white sticker. When he goes for another section, our hands accidentally touch. There's a gasp that escapes my lips without me meaning to.

He has a devilish smile on his face. He's excited to have me here all alone with the thought that I am excited and nervous for him to touch me and notice me.

"You know what, I think I could use a glass of wine. Do you want one?"

I laugh a little, "I am nowhere near being legal."

He stands giving me his hand to help lift me up, "You're very mature for your age Maggie. I think you can handle it."

The idea that he thinks of me as an adult is far too thrilling. "Okay, I'll have one."

That is where it started. It's where we started.

11

When we are all about to leave, I text Arlo that I will wait for her outside. It is mainly because I have to get some fresh air but also because I need to see him. Jamie Cartwright has not been a part of my life for quite some time and when I think of him there's this enough weight of guilt on my shoulders. He is not helping by sending secret text messages to me knowing I cannot answer him and knowing that I am with my family.

It is getting darker outside and the stars and the moon are shining so brilliantly over the town. Their sweetness drapes a cloak around the horrific sight that is this evening. The last time I went to one of these dances, I was eighteen and secretly hoping my dad would show up like he did when I was little and dance with me to his favorite song "Brown-eyed girl", but I knew better than to expect that.

I wonder what my father thought about last. I wonder if before he passed away he felt about his kids or wife. Maybe he thought about his career skyrocketing even more after he died. Perhaps he was scared? He had this way about him where when he was happy, he was the kindest and warmest person you knew, but when he was scared or angry, he was the scariest. I used to shrink at the thought of making him angry, and then somehow as I got older things changed. I was more bold and blunt and he was the one who would shrink at the thought of upsetting me.

I take a seat on the cold grass feeling it softly scratch against my skin but not caring to move. My dress is far too thin for the cold breeze hitting me but I like it. I like feeling numb.

"It's far too cold out for you to only be wearing that," Ashton's voice appears from what seems like out of nowhere.

I shake my head not looking at him, "I like it. I've always liked the cold." I hear him scoff at me and then he sits down throwing his large black coat over my shoulders. His shoulders touch mine and a spark comes back to me. Sometimes I think he feels it too. It might be a juvenile thought. Leftover feelings from a childhood crush blinded me from seeing that we're just friends, but still, it is nice to dream about what would have happened if instead of tripping over Jamie, I fell for Ashton. And then I remember the other night when he told me he didn't have a girlfriend. It was weird that he felt the need to tell me that in my room in the middle of the night. "Can I ask you a question?"

"Of course," he says.

"The other night you came over you told me you didn't have a girlfriend, why?"

I don't look into his eyes, but mine glaze over his body and he seems stiff. "I just wanted you to know."

"I talk to you on the phone with Arlo all of the time and you never corrected that before..."

"Mags," he says exasperated, "we're so different than when we were younger."

I feel myself break out with nervousness. What does that even mean? I feel like I'm exactly the same... "what does that mean?" I snapped at him.

He throws his head in his hands. "Why didn't you ever tell me how you felt back then? Why'd you get with him?" He pointed at Jamie's house and my stomach dropped. Arlo... Son of a bitch! No one was supposed to know. My mother would kill me and then Jamie.

I push myself away from him a little, "What are you talking about?"

"Please don't lie to me. I saw you two one night." I throw my hair back stressed from the thought of having this conversation with anyone but Arlo. "I was on my way home from work and the two of you were in his house on the second floor. You were laughing and I remember thinking, she's so beautiful when she laughs, and then he fucking kissed you. He kissed you like it was normal. Like he did it all of the time."

"Because he did." I don't say it because I am proud of it. I don't say it because I think we made sense. There is just something in his eyes begging me not to lie to him that I cannot ignore. "It's been over for a long time Ashton. Why are you asking me about it now?"

He closes the gap between us and the warmth from his body brings some comfort to my skin. His coat is barely helping me from freezing completely. When his hand goes for mine and our fingers lock, I wonder if it's possible to stop a moment in time. He's right. We are different than when we were younger because when he would hug me and or hold my hand back it all felt platonic but here it feels like we are coming together. We are setting a foundation for us.

I know what I want. I want him, but as much as that has remained true for years, my father just died. I'm not good at loving anyone, least of all myself. Most importantly, my head cannot take anything else that is complicated. "I can't," I say, pulling away from him. "I just cannot do this right now."

I hear him mutter something to himself, but I cannot find it in me to stay and listen to him. There's too much happening all at once for me.

Ashton knows about me and Jamie.

Ashton admitted he felt something for me.

Jamie won't leave me alone.

My father died.

My father has been writing me secret letters leading up to his death.

I know absolutely nothing about anyone in my life.

12

As everyone finishes getting ready for the party, My hands dig through the secret drawer in my dad's study until I find my next letter.

February 1, 2002
Dear Maggie,

Something terrible has happened.
You had a date.
It was not a real date since luckily for me you are only two years old, however, it has made me riddled with worry that once you get older and turn into this beautiful young woman anyone will want to be with you. Do you know what makes that thought worse? I just found out I am having another daughter! So now, I have not one but two little girls that are stunning under one roof. Heaven help me. (Not that I believe in such a fantasy land).

On a much lighter less scribbled anxiety note, your second birthday went splendidly. Your grandmother was able to make it (much to your mother's disappointment) and Taylor made me promise to have a Harry Potter birthday cake made for you since he knows he wanted one but didn't want to ask for it.

You do that a lot. You don't want to ask for things because you think you are asking for too much. You never want to seem like an inconvenience because of something embedded inside of you but I don't want that for you. I never want you to feel like an inconvenience for anyone because if you do then they are probably not the right person for you.

I want you to shine bright and if someone asks you to turn your light down, turn it up for them.

As always, Today is my favorite day because it is your birthday.

All my love,

Dad.

I feel so cold that I almost worry about a window being open in here but when I turn my head to look at the window it's shut. It makes me think of when I was little used to watching shows about ghosts. They used to say the temperature would drop when there was a ghost around.

Before I say anything, I know I am acting crazy but I just wish it were true, "Dad," I say, waiting a moment before I say anything again. "Can I tell you a secret?" The silence continues to feel like it is suffocating me. "I miss you."

I put the letter back into the secret drawer trying to keep myself from telling Reed and Taylor that I suddenly felt ill so that I could stay home and have some peace and quiet with my dad's letters. Then again, a part of me worries about what will happen once I get to the end of them. I fear that these letters will only confuse me more about who he was and more importantly who he was to me.

"Sweetheart?" Mother says as she opens the study doors. She looks stunning in her black gown and silver blazer. I could try but I doubt I would remember a time when she didn't look gorgeous. Her eyes meet mine and for once they don't look like she's about to judge me for merely existing. "Maggie, are you ready? We are about to head out."

"Yeah, I am. I just wanted a moment alone."

She sighs and I hear her whisper something like, "Otis used to want that too."

13

Arlo and I walk hand in hand into the boathouse that is currently filled with the entire town's people. Little foil stars hang from the ceiling by a thin string. The lights at each corner of the room help light them creating little star shadows on all of the walls. The sound of champagne bottles popping startled Arlo and me, making us jump and begin to laugh. I guess it can be nice being home after all.

"Castine," Arlo says, snatching champagne from a waiter, "I forgot what a classy son of a bitch she was."

"It's beautiful," I add. I look all over for Ashton hoping that Arlo thinks I am looking at the decorations again.

It doesn't fool her though because she moves a piece of hair out my face while telling me, "He told me he was running late."

"Who?"

"You can drop the act, Maggie." Music begins to play filling the space around us. Lily Braxton must be in charge of the music again this year because Coldplay's "Yellow" wouldn't be chosen by anyone else. The memory of prom still scares me. Coldplay was the only thing played for four hours and if anyone tried to change it, they were verbally assaulted. "Look, I know I freaked out but Ashton and I talked earlier."

"Oh God..." I begin to say.

She holds up a finger to silence me, "I told him about Jamie when he came to visit last time in December. I didn't mean to swear but it just came out. He was upset and angry about it for days. I begged him not to ask you about it."

"Arlo! What the hell?" I start to scream at her but when everyone's eyes fall on us I have to quiet down. The last thing I want is more drama in the town gossip group chats to be solely

focused on myself or my family. I grab her hand and we walk
outside to the pier where there are only two teenagers making
out so I assume that they don't care about what we are going to
talk about. "Why did you tell him about Jamie?"

"He told me he was in love with you and he saw you kiss
Jamie and he wanted to ignore it. He was hoping he saw it
wrong but the more he saw you the more sense it made and he
didn't know what to do so he didn't do anything. I couldn't lie
to him about it, Maggie. I didn't want to lie to him about it anyway."

He was in love with me... he loved me... He might still love
me. I feel my head spin and I grip it. "When did this get so
fucking complicated?"

She begins to rub my shoulders, "Maybe when you fucked
our married neighbor." I shove her hands off of me and she
laughs, "It's funny because it's true!"

I can't help it. I start to laugh. Crouching over I feel tears
filling my eyes. Arlo begins to fan herself with her hands. The
truth is, my life as of this moment is almost comical. The guy of
my dreams has the worst timing. My ex-fling/ neighbor will not
leave me alone. I barely know what I am doing with my life.
Lastly, I am going insane talking to my dead dad like he is still
there. There's just no redeeming moment in sight for me.

"Sweetie," Arlo says, "I get it if you are not ready to be with
someone right now, but I would hate it if you just pushed someone away because you were scared."

"Me too." I hear the sounds of Prince starting to play letting
me know my mom, Taylor, and Reed have arrived because they
are the only three people that request Prince in this town of old
lady librarians. "We should probably go inside now."

"I guess you're right."

I take her arm and she leads me to the middle of the dance floor where Taylor and Reed are dancing inside a circle of onlookers. Taylor is working on his version of the sprinkler while Reed is solely focused on mating calls pointed at a stunning blonde with blue eyes in a hunter-green gown.

I don't bother being embarrassed by them, instead, I run in the middle of the circle with them and do my version of the chicken dance. Arlo glows red but I know she adores my excellent chicken dance moves.

"The Honors trio!" Reed shouts.

"The Honors trio!" Taylor and I yell in unison.

14

One thing that is important to note when it comes to all of the Honors children is that while we are different, the one thing we have in common is a severe problem with commitment. Taylor dates, but his longest relationship was about four months. Reed does this thing where she loves to be in love but it becomes her whole personality to the point that around one year into her relationships she claims they went too fast (even though that is the pace she set herself) and ultimately breaks up with them. I, on the other hand, just don't date. Dating has always been this thing that in theory sounds great but actually being with someone who has the opportunity to get to know me sounds terrifying. All of this is important information because as I am dancing with Arlo and my brother on the dance floor and I notice Ashton walking my way I decide the best thing to do is literally run away from my problems.

I am currently still running.

I had to take off my heels and hold them because there is no way I could run with them on. The pavement is wet from the rain that poured down on Castine earlier and the feeling that I might possibly slip and die is well known to me. My throat is dried out but I have no energy in me to be concerned about my rough breathing. Each light post that I pass is a reminder that I am going insane. I could have asked anyone in this town for a ride home and they would have done so, but I didn't take a moment to think of logical ways to solve my avoidance problem.

Finally! My house comes into view for me, but as I get closer I see the fairlady, Ashton's car, in my driveway. I stop in the middle of the street, stunned that he somehow got here before me. Now that I think about it, an old lady could have crawled to my house before I got there by from the boathouse.

He notices me in the middle of the street and rushes out of his car. "So," he yells slamming his door shut, "You would rather run all of the way home in the dark than talk to me about your feelings?"

"Um," I say, trying to think of the perfect thing to say, "I wasn't feeling well..."

"Would you please just let me talk to you in your house instead of in the middle of the street?"

I don't bother fighting him because I can tell from the crease in between his eyebrows he's frustrated with me. I know that I have not been fair to a lot of people recently. I haven't been fair to Ashton when it comes to his feelings for me. I haven't been fair to Jamie's wife and kids with all of the lies I have told over the years. I certainly wasn't fair to my family when I packed up my life and never came back home. I just want to be a better person to people.

Ashton and I walked up the steps to my front door together. When we get inside, I throw my heels on the floor and then snatch Ashton's hand leading him up the stairs to my room.

My room is a mess with all of the clothes in here from when Taylor and Reed got ready in here with me earlier. I do not care that much so I just shove everything off of my bed so that we can sit on it together. He sits across from me, his brown hair tousled around wildly, and he attempts to speak to me.

"I've had feelings for you pretty much my entire life," I tell him.

"You never said anything to me," he replies, "I just thought you wanted to be friends."

"You didn't tell me how you felt either."

He takes a moment and then says, "I knew I loved you when you stopped coming by the coffee house after school."

The day that Jamie started was the end of when I did things outside of him and school. I stopped going by the coffeehouse to study, I stopped swimming for school, I stopped doing a lot of things that mattered to me because I was so consumed by Jamie.

"Jamie," I tell him like it answers all of his questions.

"That is the thing," he says pointing at me, "I do not understand that at all. You're this strong, prideful, intelligent person and he's the definition of creepy. I don't understand how that even worked."

"It didn't work." My heart feels like it might explode but for once I need to be honest. "I know it is hard to understand and I do not think I fully understood it until just now but I felt so alone and so unloved that it didn't matter who showed me affection. He caught me at the wrong time and if you had told me how you felt back then unfortunately I think you would have also caught me at a bad time. He used me as an excuse for his loveless marriage. I don't want to be someone's excuse; I want to be their everything." I don't think I realized how good it would feel to honestly explain how I used to see myself and how I still do sometimes, but now that it is out in the open; I feel good that my life is starting to make some sense.

Slowly, his fingers intertwined with mine and he whispered close to my face, "Whenever you are ready to let me prove you are everything to me, let me know."

He begins to leave, but I keep a hold of him begging him silently to stay. I don't like to be alone right now especially if I have the option to keep him here with me. "Would you stay with me? I want to show you something."

His deep green eyes widen with the offer and then he smiles his ever-so-attractive smile and says, "Of course." He takes off his winter coat and throws it on my bed. I ask him to follow me downstairs to show him the letters.

Arlo and Ashton are now going to be the two people who know about the letters because I need to have people to talk about them with, but I cannot tell my family yet. I need to know what that last letter says before I do that.

In the study, the darkness consumed the space except for the golden hugh from his lamp on the far end of his desk. "Close the door," I ask him.

"Why are we in the dark in your father's study?" He asks reluctantly, shutting the doors shut.

"I want you to see something," I sit on the chair and pull the drawer open. Once I hit the latch to reveal the loose bottom, Ashton was amazed.

"What the hell?" He asks.

"I found them when I got home."

15

Ashton sat there stunned on my bed after we left the study, caught off guard by my father's words he kept a secret until after his death.

I have changed into my bunny pajamas which I wasn't self-conscious of until now. Ashton is lying in my bed in his shirt and boxers and on any other night, I would think something might happen between us, but this is an odd situation for that.

"So," he says, "I thought I would have something to say by now, but I don't."

I laugh a little and then lay down next to him, "Now you know how I have been feeling for the past few days ."

My favorite thing about my room is the way the noise in the house does not seem to reach my room. It's on the second floor and at the farthest end of the hall where the attic is right above me. Sometimes the silence was too much but with Ashton here, it is a welcoming thought that we're all alone. I move his arm so that it is on my waist and then I move my leg over him. The smell of vanilla hits me and it is intoxicating. Ashton has always been intoxicating to me.

"Mags," he says, kissing the top of my head making my eyes roll, "Do you miss him?"

"Yeah," I reply, trying not to cry, "I have never been good at admitting stuff like that, but I do. I think I have been missing him my whole life."

"What do you mean?"

I sigh, "When I was really young, he was my favorite person. We stayed up late, he read me his stories and I read him mine, we played hide and seek, he taught me about Jane Austin and Agatha Christie, and he let me hide candy from my mom so if I wanted some I could grab it from our secret place and he wouldn't tell her."

He plants another sweet kiss on the top of my head, "When did he stop being your favorite person?"

"When he started putting his books out. They always seemed more important than me or Taylor and Reed. He stopped buying my mom flowers and surprising her with date nights. They fought all of the time over something stupid like what color pants she bought me for the holiday card. He became this on-the-surface person instead of the deep-loving man I used to know. I never knew why."

"But the letters might tell you."

"Yeah, they might. I am just scared of learning something I don't want to know."

He squeezes my hip making my thoughts run wild of what it would be like for him to touch me everywhere. "Nothing good ever came from someone not knowing the truth."

"I guess you're right. Maybe if we just told each other how we felt back then I wouldn't have gotten with the creepy neighbor."

It is a joke but he doesn't take it like one. His body tenses, "He should be in jail," he whispers as if I wouldn't hear him, "He... hurt you."

"Ashton, I am fine. It was just a mistake."

"Waiting for a vulnerable young woman to be in a place where she thinks having a relationship with a grown man is normal is predatory."

"I know, but that's not something we need to talk about right now."

"I know," he says.

He cups my face with his hands so that I am looking up at him. I am lost in him again just like I used to be when I was ten years old and he played basketball on his front lawn. He's always been my Ashton in my dreams and now it is something that might happen for me.

He gets a little closer to face and I can tell there is some hesitation from him but I can't take it anymore, "If you don't kiss me now, then I am afraid that I might explode."

"You've always had a way with words haven't you?" He says mischievously before his lips crash into me.

My hands go into his hair pulling and tugging on his chocolate curls while his lips continuously play with my own. When I arch my neck back my mouth opens a little and a moan escapes my lips. I feel him smile against my mouth. He seems proud of making me feel anything when it comes to him- making me want him especially.

His hands go to the hem of my shift and then underneath it. His warmth stuns my cool stomach, making me jump. When he laughs a little I think of the first time Jamie touched me. I think about how intense it felt crossing over into something foreign with him when he'd only been a family friend at that point. This doesn't feel foreign or strange at all. This feels like I am finally coming home.

His hips start to move against mine and I feel that he wants me to without even looking at him. Once his lips begin to roll down my neck he whispers against it, "Maybe we should take it slow..."

I could punch him for saying such a thing, "I think ten-plus years is slow enough don't you?" I sound eager and strange, I might be embarrassed but not with him. Never with him.

"I cannot argue with such intelligent reasoning."

My lips started to move further and further down my body and with that so did my ability to think about anything at all. His fingers found their way to my pink fluffy pajama pants sliding them down my legs with such ease I was dying with anticipation. It was too hard for me to wait so I yanked my shirt off myself and threw it on the ground next to where Ashton threw my pajama pants.

When I am fully naked, he just hovers over me for a moment. I reach for him but he laughs and rubs the tattoo that is on my hip, "You have a Deathly Hallows tattoo on your hip? Why is that such a turn-on?"

"Well, good taste is attractive," I replied.

He laughs softly as he rests his body on top of me. I no longer feel chilly because Ashton is on top of me. The heat from the two of our bodies together is so inebriating I could get drunk on the feeling. His lips collide with mine once more and I take the chance to run my hands down and unbutton his pants greedily freeing him.

He rubs against me making me moan, "Shh baby," I cannot hide my smile from him calling me baby, "I would prefer to not have to explain this to your mother." His right hand covers my mouth while the other helps steady him against me and in a quick motion he thrusts inside me, sending me close to the edge. Sex, kissing, and just being around someone has never felt this good with anyone but Ashton. I don't know anyone that could make me feel like this nor do I want to know.

My grip on his arm gets tighter as we keep moving together. Instead of keeping his hand covering my mouth, he moves it swiftly and his tongue is inside swirling my own making me wince with the pleasure he brings me.

"Fuck," he says as I lift my hips to meet him adequately, "I am trying to make this last longer, but if you do shit like that, I will combust."

"That," I say, kissing him, "Is," another kiss, "The point."

He grips my face tightly kissing me as he comes undone with myself joining him. "I can't believe I even tried to do that with someone else."

I can't believe it either.

I open my eyes thinking that I must have slept in because my light is turned on again. When we were little and we had to get up for school, my mom would turn on the light and tell us good morning. If we tried to sleep some more she would flicker the light on and off. For a moment, I worry that's what's happening so I jump awake but then I notice no one is in my room, not even my... boyfriend. Is that what he's called now?

I look at the clock on my desk and see that it's only 2 a.m. Where could he have gone? Did he not want to see me? I don't even know what's happening or if last night was just some erotic dream I will think about endlessly.

Suddenly the door opens and Ashton appears. He catches me with his eyes and a sweet smirk appears on his face letting me relax finally. "Uh, Arlo knows we slept together..." he doesn't sound embarrassed. He actually sounds a little thrilled. Studying him some more, I can tell he's hopping from side to side excited.

"Why are you doing that?"

"Because I am happy and happy people like to hop."

"Do happy people like to get back in bed and hold the naked girl they just had sex with?"

"Of course they do," he climbs into bed with me, moving his hands over my stomach and in between my thighs making me squirm a little. "I am deeply sorry we haven't done that before now."

My eyes feel heavy again but I have to tell him, "You should be."

16

"Gross!" Arlo screams.

"Would you keep your voice down?" I shout out at her as I open my dad's study.

Ashton left early this morning to go home and hopefully be there before his dads and Arlo woke up. His plan did not go well, because when he opened his front door Arlo was waiting patiently in the living room fuming over Ashton never coming home and his location showing him across the street.

I was hoping to have some more time alone in our little bubble, stuck in a romantic haze before we would have to explain what we are to everyone. Some things have changed like us admitting how we feel and when we started feeling it; however, some things have not changed. I'm still the worst with my emotions and relationships and my dad is still dead haunting me beyond the grave with words that don't weigh as much as they would if he were alive.

"I'm not saying I'm not happy for you but like you fucked my brother that's weird. What if I fucked your brother?"

"That would be weird."

"Exactly!" She shouts!

"Arlo, shut up! I don't want to be interrupted." The floor was so cold from the harsh winter and my mother needed to have the AC on at all times so my feet lightly hopped to my dad's desk. I didn't think to put on some slippers, I just knew what I needed- more letters. What happened with Ashton felt so unreal and I think that is partly because I never felt real. I always felt like this odd two-dimensional person. I always felt like a side character on a sitcom you never saw again and never cared enough to ask about. Ashton makes me wonder if I have been looking at my life all wrong and why on earth my parents made me feel that way at all.

I pull the following letter from my father on my third birthday reading it quietly to myself first before Arlo whispers angrily, "Read it out loud whore!"

February 1, 2003
Dear Maggie,
This year on your birthday my love I had to call you.

Some amazing things happened this year like us finding out you are going to have a little sister in May and your mom opening her own gallery huge things happened this year like my book selling to a movie production company.

I always wanted to give you kids the life you deserved and not the life that I had, which was giving my dad rent money at the age of seventeen and wondering what we should do; rent or Christmas? I wanted you guys to think about what presents to ask for and choose between your top three colleges and this will definitely ensure that.

I sold the movie rights for a hundred thousand dollars which I used to create college funds for all of you and give to your mom to help with her gallery. Everything I have ever done is for you and your brother. It just breaks my heart that I am not with you today. I called you the second the clock struck midnight for me even though it was ten for you. The sound of your tears will genuinely haunt me forever and I fear that it might be the death of me if I have to hear it again.

The Barbie Dream House and book of the month subscription hopefully helps you forget how awful it is that your busy dad wasn't there this morning with birthday waffles covered in whipped cream and sprinkles.

Just please know that I am hurting too because today is my favorite day also known as your birthday.

Love you to the moon and to Saturn,

Dad.

"The moon and Saturn," Arlo says, "That is always what you tell me."

She is right. It is something that I used to tell Taylor and Reed when I tucked them into bed at night too. If they were scared or crying I used to get the star lights that made their ceiling glow and tell them, "I love you to the moon and to Saturn."

"Cross your heart," Taylor would say.

"It's crossed."

"It's just something I used to say to everyone. I guess now that I think about it my dad used to say it to me and Taylor and Reed."

The moon and Saturn were not the only exciting things about this letter. It also gave me a time frame. This is when the missing things started. It is when he began thinking that material things mattered more than actually having our dad around. Back then seeing him just in the summer felt like Christmas and when it was Christmas having all of those presents under the tree felt like a knife to all of their backs.

But he still said that her birthday was his favorite day...

"It was not here." She said clutching the paper with Arlo leaning over her at the desk.

"What was not there?"

"The break. The moment when everything changed between us." My hand touched my collarbone playing with the lines on my chest just to have something to do.

Arlo started to rub the top of my head with her hand, gently moving back and forth on my scalp to ease my comfort. "Do you really think that if you keep reading these letters there is going to be a part where he says, this is the moment I stopped loving you?"

"I don't know, maybe, or maybe not. It would just be nice to have some answers. I would love to know why he decided I wasn't good enough to be his daughter anymore or why I wasn't good enough to show up. What could I have done to make him not love me anymore?"

I didn't notice it, but I started to cry. Arlo's fingers wipe away the tears for me several times before she kisses the top of my forehead and says, "Children shouldn't have to beg their parents to make them feel good enough; if you do then I think it was simply just bad parenting. It is on him and on Val that you guys didn't feel loved by your parents. It's got nothing to do with any of you."

"I know that in theory, just not in reality."

There's a soft knock at the door making me jump. I bang my elbow on the desk as someone enters, I shove the letters into the false bottom hoping whoever enters doesn't suspect anything. I need this to stay a secret for now. It needs to be my secret.

A curious Taylor enters with a smile on his face. Arlo and I visibly relax because Taylor being Taylor would have immediately asked questions if he thought something was off. He is still in his pajamas and white shirt dressed nicely with his messy brown hair. "Pull-Out is here with Dad's lawyer to do the will."

"The will?" Arlo asks.

I completely forgot. My father's will which I am sure I am not on will most likely just consist of dad's money and who gets the house which is my mother's obviously. "Okay, I will be right out."

"Okay, just hurry! I want Pull-Out to leave as soon as possible!"

Arlo laughs a little once the door is closed causing me to ask her, "What is so funny?"

"He wants him to pull out."

"That is terrible," I add, "We can't use that."

17

Everyone in the room is still in their pajamas due to the fact that it is only nine in the morning, except by no surprise my mother. Her hair is perfectly slicked back into a bun shining like a mirrorball. Her white pantsuit with gold buttons looks like she is ready for a press day for a movie she is starring in.

It is something that she cannot help. If there is company coming, then everything must be pristine. My dad was not that way at all and it infuriated her. They would be having neighbors over for dinner and my mom would spend hours making sure nothing was out of place and all of their wedding china was out, but my dad would be in the backyard with a book or his notebook and pin just enjoying the day. He could care less what anyone thought of his house or his clothes. I really respected him back then and I guess that is something else within myself I might have gotten from him.

Ryanne Mackenzie snaps his fingers loudly grabbing everyone's attention, "So," he yells from the green velvet chair across the couch, "I understand it is a lovely winter day and we just need to get through this so you all can go back to mourning. Might I say I am so sorry for your loss?"

"Are you really?" I replied.

Mother sends me daggers in her eyes but I ignore her. I am truly tired of people just saying they are sorry for my loss when they genuinely couldn't care any less.

"Anyway," he says pulling out a large envelope, "Let's get started huh? Obviously, Mrs. Honors, you know what is in here and I am sure that information has been shared with your children.

"That would require us to have a better relationship I'm afraid," I say which now makes Taylor eye me down fiercely.

Enough he mouths from the floor by mother.

"Otis was very clear about how he wanted his assets to be divided up between his family. The very first thing that he wanted was to have his mother nowhere near the reading of his will because the only thing she can have is the house he helped her buy."

Reed begins to giggle, "Oh Grandma."

"This house; however, is given to Taylor."

We all stop to look at each other. The perfect house isn't going to his perfect wife?

Taylor stands up looking slightly ill. His skin is pale and he seems to be sweating, "What do you mean he is leaving me the house?"

"To the best of my understanding, this has been yours since you were eighteen."

"It's true," mother adds. "We always thought it was best to leave it to one of you kids and Taylor you are the only one who showed any interest in this place."

"But what if I don't want it?" He asks her.

"It is not like you have to have it, you can sell it if you want preferably not while I am alive but there you go."

"How about we move on?" Pull-out says.

I sit back on the couch sipping my coffee knowing damn well there is nothing this will do for me. I spent most of my teenage years fucking my neighbor right under his nose and he didn't know a damn thing and that was because he didn't pay much attention to me. Even when I was at college, our relationship felt the exact same. Usually, parents feel a need to check on their kids a little more since they are not seeing them all of the time. My Dad didn't see me regardless of our living arrangements so my being away didn't do any more damage.

"The next thing is the trust funds that he set up for all of you which still remain at the same value of 100,000 dollars each which you all may access at any time now that he has passed."

That part we all knew about. I never touched it because I didn't want him to think I needed his money but seeing as he is now gone I guess I could use it to buy a condo in New York after I graduate or just let it grow in savings.

"The next is his movie production company that he uses to produce his book adaptations and be a producer in up-and-coming projects. This will go to Mrs. Honors as discussed prior to his death last year. His cars such as the Audie and Impala will go to his youngest daughter Reed."

"Sweet," Reed says.

"Lastly his publishing company will go to his eldest Daughter Margaret."

The words are too unbelievable I don't even realize that he just said that. I ignored it as if it didn't happen because I must have misheard him. There's simply no way Dad would have trusted me with anything let alone his legacy. His most prized possession and passion in his life- his writing.

"Maggie, did you hear him, honey?"

Her question makes me understand that I am wrong. That did just happen after all. He left me his publishing company. The thing that he created out of nothing. Honors Publishing located right here in Maine was now mine.

My throat gets a little dry and unsure how to proceed I simply say, "I... I heard him."

Mother smiles and waves her left hand letting the light shine off of her expensive wedding ring. The emerald shines just like it did the day my dad got it for her. Looking at it makes me out of sorts knowing he probably thought the ring, his company, his cars, and pretty much everything he owned was the legacy he was leaving behind instead of his kids.

"I am so sorry; I need to be excused."

Taylor tries to grab my hand, but I shake it off of me and pull open the front door forcefully. When I slam it shut, I hear a picture fall off the wall and shatter on the floor. My heart begins to beat too fast and much like many times in my life before this moment, I run. I don't have a phone or my house key, but the thought of being in that house right now makes me feel as though I am being crushed to death.

This time is different because I don't run across town in freezing weather for long. Before I know it, I run across the street to the one home in this entire town I consider to be functional- the Cunninghams.

I knock heavily on the bright oak door three times. Mr. Cunningham opens it with a smile on his face unaware of my current mood, "Maggie, come on in!" I move past him and smell the chocolate chip cookies in the oven. He is a quiet and sweet man. His favorite thing to do in life is bake cookies. It doesn't matter what time of the year or what they are supposed to be for baking made him happy. The other Mr.Castle is more like me. Ryder liked to be opinionated and free. He is much more mature and emotionally stable, but still, we connect on a lot of things.

Arlo and Ashton were adopted pretty young so they are the only people that are their parents in their minds. They never cared that they weren't biologically real to their dads because it didn't matter. I used to wish I would feel that way about my parents.

"Do you mind if I go up and talk to Ash or Arlo?" I ask him.

"Arlo isn't home yet. She and Ryder are at the store but Ashton is up there!"

"Thank you!"

I run up the stairs too harshly making my feet hit the wood loudly. If I were Ashton I would be worried about someone coming to kill me. I make it to his room push his door open and find him shirtless and on the phone with someone. He looks at me concerned. His sweet soft smile fades into a thin line and then he says into the phone, "Arlo just get the grocery store pie for dinner." He hangs up and throws his phone at the end of his bed.

I don't take much time to tell him why I'm here, "I... I don't know what to do."

He swings his legs over the edge of his bed and pats the space next to him asking me to sit down. "I knew I came on too strong."

"Oh no! It's not that at all! My dad, we read the Will and he left me something and I'm not sure why."

I sit down and finally feel some warmth, not heat to heal me from the freezing cold outside but the warmth from the nicest feeling of having someone to go to.

"You see, I am torn here because the last time I tried to mention your father you ran away from me but as someone who would like to be your boyfriend at some point I am feeling the need to help you talk about your father again."

I try really hard to ignore the fact that he just said he wants to be my boyfriend and focus. Focus on the fact that he is here for me at this moment. My golden retriever boy is too stunning.

"He left me his publishing company."

"That was... unexpected."

"Why would he do such a thing?"

Ashton stands up and throws on his sweater from his laundry pile in the corner, "Let's find out."

<u>18</u>

When I was fifteen my grandfather died the day before Christmas.

It was difficult because I didn't know him. I knew my grandmother Sharon who despite being a mean old hag was lovely when I wore the sweaters she bought for me for Christmas. Grandpa Cain was different.

I didn't know until I was older but he used to hit my father as a child. He used to beat him so often that my dad thought it was normal. Boys are just being boys and all that.

When my dad met my mom however she refused to let my dad think that way. She begged him to listen to her and understand that's not how parents show love and after a little while he understood. He also made the decision to stop speaking to him. He helped with money from time to time but other than that they had no relationship.

We went to Texas for the funeral and there were maybe ten people there including my father's half-sister whom he only saw on his Facebook page. They looked alike with their dark features and pale skin but she was so much taller than him and she had these little brown dots on her skin that my dad didn't have. When we walked into the church to take a seat, she waved at him and smiled. He smiled back but it was one of those fake grins that people do when they are walking past someone in a hallway. He smiled like she was a familiar stranger.

"Lenora," Mother whispered to him, "If she comes over here understand I don't play nice."

He kissed her cheek and then told her, "I love you."

He grabbed Reed's hand Mother held mine and Taylor led us to the pew to take our seats. My fingers traced the outline of the drawing etched into the wood. It was a cross. I remember rubbing it the entire time waiting for the funeral to be over. I have never been good with people dying because if you are too sad when you don't really know them then it feels wrong, but if you are not sad enough, then you are not being compassionate.

"Dad," I remember asking him, "why didn't we spend more time with Grandpa?"

He leaned over and whispered as the priest came to the podium and welcomed everyone to church, "Because I love you too much."

"What does that even mean?" Mom glared at me which she did whenever she thought I went too far.

"Cain was not a very good person to me and I do not want my little girl alone with a man like that." He kissed my forehead and I knew the conversation was over.

After the priest was done speaking, everyone piled into their cars getting in line to go to the burial except for us. We got into Dad's rental car and drove in the opposite direction.

It was cold in Texas, not as bad as Maine, but it was still far too chilly. My black turtleneck was too thin and I spilled coke on my jacket in the gathering room at the church which made it even worse.

Even back then I felt like in Winter, no one really felt alive. Least of all my father.

19

February 1, 2004

Dear Maggie,

Today is your birthday therefore it needs to be all about you which is why when your grandfather called to tell me he wanted to see you because he deserved to at 3 in the morning, I threw our landline into the fireplace.

Your mom always says that the reason why people might have blowups and tantrums is that keeping things inside can only work for so long. And when it comes to Cain, I do not tell you kids everything. You all know that I was born and raised in Texas. You know that I went to Trinity High School not that any of this means anything to you yet because your main focus is how long you can hold your breath until you are no longer certain you will live. I do still tell you everything that I think you should know because when you get older and you remember your life as a child, I want it to be filled with memories where I talk to you all like adults because that is who I am raising- adults. You all are going to be older one day with your own lives and be telling your own kids what kind of person you are and who you were before they got there and like me some stuff you might want to leave out so I will tell you in this letter what I will not tell you out loud when you are this young.

Your Grandfather abused me.

I think I was your age when it first happened. My mom and dad had just gotten a divorce and Cain was an awful mess of a person. He moped about the house and when he was not doing that he was drinking. I love my mom but to this day I still do not understand why he left me with him if she knew how he was.

Anyway, I had come into the living room and was excited to show him the story I had just written and he was watching TV. I guess I was just bothering him so when I yelled for him he turned around and smacked me so hard that he left a mark on my cheek for a couple of days.

I think growing up with someone like that in a situation where we were so poor and always together made me think of how I wanted to be a parent. It is why I work so hard to make a good living so that your kids do not have to worry. It is why I send your mother flowers once a week even if we just had a fight and it is also why you or your siblings will never be alone with that man.

The three of you are pieces of my heart living and breathing in the outside world, and my father has already proved to me he doesn't care about breaking my heart.

Please know all I think about is not breaking yours.

I love you, my little moon.

Today as always is my favorite day...

Dad

Ashton stops reading it and sets the letter down on my bed. We are both too shocked to say anything to each other at first. It was just silent with only the sound of the rain that began shortly before we started reading the letter to fill the space.

"Did you know?" Ashton asks, motioning towards the letter.

"I knew about it a little bit but hearing about it like that makes me want to vomit."

He grabs my hand and squeezes it, "I think your father loved you more than anything."

"But why did he leave all of the time? Why make me feel like shit for barely existing? It doesn't make sense..."

"I am not sure, but I don't think he was this villain that hated his children. Maybe he just forgot about what matters the most..."

Someone knocks gently on my door and before they walk in I think about pulling my hand away, but I don't. It feels right to acknowledge this as something that is blossoming. If I didn't have Ashton in my life during a moment like this, I am not sure I would be considered sane. Reed is the one to enter holding the keys to Dad's Impala.

Reed and Dad had a special relationship because when she was born he would say things like "This is my free spirit," and "That is my unicorn," he knew she had something different about her. It was why when she wanted tattoos he said she should get them and why when she said she was a lesbian he said that he didn't care. Reed was always Reed, her own special kind of person, and every single one of us loves that.

The first thing she ever asked my dad to do for her was let her sit in his lap as he drove around the neighborhood in the Impala or as she called it at the time "Paula". He taught her how to change a flat and use a grill. I never thought to ask for any of that but she did and he loved having things to show her. That is why I am not at all surprised that he left her his car. He loved those things and Reed would be the only person to love them as much as he did.

"Anyone up for a ride in Paula."

"He left you his car?" Ashton says thrilled.

Reed shakes her head, "Good old Otis. He knew leaving them to Mom would mean their demise."

Our mother drives much like her parents; hoping for the best but still getting in the wrong lane every time she makes a move. "We'll meet you downstairs in five minutes," I tell her. She closes the door and I hear her skip down the hallway before I say something. "I have to know where these letters take me before they find out about them. Taylor and Reed were not like me. It didn't matter how flawed our parents were, they stayed in Castine to be with Mom and Dad. I have to protect them."

Ashton nods his head, "When are you going to let someone protect you?"

I smile because I can't help it and pull his face to mine. We begin to kiss softly, allowing our bodies to rock back and forth. "I think I am getting there just fine with you," I whisper.

20

The Impala is old, not old like it cannot drive, aged like the heater stopped working ten years ago and we couldn't get it fixed because it's hard to find that part made for this car. This is a crucial detail to know about because when Reed asked us to go for a drive, we forgot about the damn heater.

Castine's bitter cold is enjoyable when you are inside cuddled up with a blanket and the fireplace but when you are driving down the road at sixty miles an hour with only your jacket for warmth- it's torture.

"Reed, cool it!" I scream at her as we zoom past our old high school, "I am fucking freezing!"

"Maggie! Live a little!" She slams her foot down on the accelerator and we kick up to eighty miles an hour. My face is officially frozen and there seems to be no moisture in my mouth.

The impala goes past the beach and I remember something I must have forgotten a long time ago... I always wanted to do something crazy like jump in the water in the freezing cold. It is a tradition from my mom's side of the family to jump into a frozen lake. My grandmother told us that a long time ago, their family dabbled in natural medicine, and the cold water was meant to rejuvenate your body and wash away bad energy. I never did it because the idea of being in a swimsuit in December was ridiculous but not so much now.

My dad's problem with life was that he didn't tell us what we meant to him when he was here. He didn't go out and have fun and not worry so much about what he should be doing versus what he wanted to do. I am not sure what my life is supposed to be, but I do know now that I want to die knowing I lived my life with no regrets.

"Reed," I say, grabbing her hand on the steering wheel, "Take the turn for the beach!"

"Alright freak," she makes a dangerously sharp turn, and then we park at the edge of the beach where the concrete pebbles meet the sand.

"What are we doing at the beach? I'm fucking freezing!" Ashton screams at us.

The thing about having a life-changing moment in the car with people, not in tune with your inner monologue is that they have no idea why you suddenly decide to do anything. It is not sudden to you. For you, every year you drove past the beach you wondered if this year would be the year you had some courage to jump into the deep end.

Reed stops the car laughing and I almost roll out of it. Ashton gets out with me and runs as well but not because he also wants to jump in instead because he has no idea what I am doing and neither do I- but I am going to do it anyway.

I reach the water and grab my boots first. Throwing them off onto the sand, I hear Reed yell at me from the car, "You moron! You are going to get sick!"

"I know!" I yell back at her.

I rip my jeans off and my sweater and run into the icy water before I change my mind.

The second I am fully submerged and feeling the water- I regret everything! My skin is so cold I think I might become paralyzed and drown. The water begins to wrap around me more, but Ashton comes to my rescue. He quickly scoops me up and helps me to shore.

"What the fuck Maggie?" He shouts at me as he throws me my clothes. We rush to get dressed together and I hear the sound of our clattering teeth becoming a shivering harmony.

As we run back to the car I begin to smile. It was a ridiculous thing to do especially since we didn't have any towels or heat packs nearby like my family usually does, but I felt terrific knowing for once I wasn't scared to do something wild with my life.

21

"Maggie honey," Mom says as she enters my room. Her eyes glance over the whole room and then she leans over a bit to look under my bed. I am about to ask why when she says, "Simply making sure you are all alone in here."

"Please do me a favor and bite me," I snap at her while looking at my television.

"Well, I just wanted to check on you since you tried to end your life earlier."

I am my mother's daughter when it comes to having a flair for the dramatic. As much as I hate having to hear her do it, I have a tendency to do the same. I simply roll my eyes at her, "I was not trying to do that! I just wanted to jump in the ocean in the freezing cold like I always wanted to do when I was younger."

She flips her perfectly done hair over her shoulder and I notice her earrings. She is wearing the teal ones Dad gave her for their first anniversary. I always wanted to wear them but she never let me. They were too special. "I wanted to also check in with you about the publishing company. You seemed distraught when you heard about it."

If by distraught she means entirely out of my mind then yes I would agree. "I just don't understand why he would leave me anything..."

She takes a seat next to me making sure to not put her shoes on my mattress. Her body language is so cold and cautious. I can tell coming in here to talk to me was something she thought about not doing at all. "Do you ever think about having kids of your own someday?"

"Why would you ask me that?"

She sighs then continues with her train of thought, "I never thought I would have any."

"Why did you?" I always wanted to ask her why. Why would someone so cold and calculated who hated the idea of a child touching her precious Prada bag give birth to three kids? It never made much sense to me.

"I was so young and so angry at the world. I hated that my life was laid out for me by your grandparents and when I met your father all of those emotions just sort of mixed into a melting pot of rebelling angst. I did realize however that I didn't want a white picket fence with three kids with anyone; I wanted it with Otis. I wouldn't have been able to do this with just anyone. He loved you all so fiercely and maybe it was not the way you wanted or how you wanted it, but he did it the best way he knew how. You're sitting here wondering why your father would leave you with something so important then I urge you to think about what you received from him."

"Taylor got the house because he's Taylor and he will use it to make a family." She shook her head yes. "Reed got the cars because she's a free spirit and always is going somewhere." I had to really think about it and even when I did nothing came to mind. "I honestly do not know."

"He loved books so much and that is why he was so successful. Books actually meant something to him so he left his company to the person he knew who felt the same way. He left it to his eldest daughter whom he used to share literature."

The time in my life when my father and I used to sit together in his study downstairs and he would read to me seems like such a long time ago almost like another lifetime. My dad loved the classics like Bronte and Jane Austin but he truly loved murder mysteries like Agatha Christie. They were his passions and when he would read them to me his eyes would light up at each plot twist thrown at us.

"I have no idea how to run a company or if I want to."

"I think that you have some time. I don't mind running everything if that is what you want. Just promise me that you will think about it some more before you give your final say?"

"I promise."

She leans over and kisses me on the cheek before getting up and leaving. Before she closes the door she pops back in and says, "I like the way Ashton looks at you. I always have."

I like the way he looks at me too.

22

February 1, 2005
Dear Maggie,
Something beautiful happened today... You read to me.
It was midnight when you came down the stairs and peered into my study with her stuffed butterfly toy in your hand. I was busy typing my new manuscript I am severely behind but you walked right in and asked me to read you, Nancy Drew. I pulled the book from my bottom shelf where I keep all of your books so that you can reach them and then I thought that it would be adorable if I made you read to me for once.

I pulled you onto my lap and handed you the book and you got so nervous I felt you shrinking inside yourself but I wanted you to have something special like reading by yourself soon if that is what you wanted. It took you only a minute to begin reading out loud proudly and it brought me so much joy. You never surprise me with your greatness; you only remind me how extraordinary you are.

It is a beautiful thing to watch your child grow into a beautiful young person and every year I take a moment and realize how lucky I am that you, Taylor, and Reed are all my kids.

I hope that one day you get to experience that too,
As always, today is my favorite day because it is your birthday.

Love you, my little moon,
Dad.

I love you, he tells me.
Your birthday is my favorite day, he tells me.
You mean everything to me, he tells me.

I begin to tear up again and don't bother to stop myself from letting myself feel the absence of the man it seems I didn't get to know. Maybe I did know him when he was like this, and I just do not remember it, or perhaps I misread him this whole time. Maybe I have had no idea what I am talking about and never have.

I miss him.

When Taylor told me that Dad died, it almost didn't feel real. It hurt, obviously, but it felt like when you hear a celebrity passed away that you loved. Did you know them? No. Did it hurt as much as it does the people that knew personally? Of course not. I know I loved my father because he was my father and I know that I love my mother because she is my mother but I think a long time ago I just stopped considering them close to my heart until now.

Being back home as an adult versus being a teenager is just different. Reading these letters and feeling what he felt for me feels different.

What if my whole life I could have just been a better daughter to him? What if we could have been better to each other and when I went to the funeral that day I could have felt everything I have started to feel since then? What if I could have told him goodbye?

I know that I shouldn't, but I grab another letter in the hopes it might make me feel better for being a piece of shit daughter.

February 1, 2006
Dear Maggie,

As I am writing this letter, I am currently on a plane to Maine attempting to be home by the time you wake up for your birthday. My little girl is six years old today and I know what I got you is perfect- a typewriter.

The thing about writing on a computer or a piece of paper is that they get the job done but there is just no magic in it. When I was younger, I had this classic typewriter. It was an olive green color and my dad got it for me after I begged him for it all year. I wrote my first story on it when I was ten about a vampire farmer who loved to eat birds. While it was pretty dramatic it is still something that I am proud of. I want you to explore all of the thoughts inside of your head and put them onto paper confidently.

When I told your mom about it, she was so mad! She hates that every year I get you a better gift than she did. Not that her gifts are not thoughtful and fun but they are! This year she got you a barbie dream house and you love Barbies. I just want you to have something that says we know you. I know that you are going to grow up into a beautiful young lady. I also know that I can't wait to see it.

Your siblings also got you something this year. Taylor worked hard to make you a poem about how you are annoying but pretty (I thought it was thoughtful) and Reed made you a picture of a sheep with cotton balls that says she is the best sister ever. Don't worry you read that right- Reed is the best sister ever, not you. You kids are indeed my main source of comedy.

I can't wait to see you, moon!

As always, today is my favorite day because it is your birthday!

Love, Dad.

Every time I think I have some answers, I just get more confused.

23

Breakfast takes place early this morning due to Mother wanting us all to go to Castine High for Dad's memorial tribute. I was prepared for this day before I even packed my bag to come home, but still, it worries me. The thought of being stuck in my old high school surrounded by teenagers who not only do not care about my father but are also being forced to sit through the tribute is downright awful. Mother planned the whole thing while her part planner handled the funeral (that is the right funeral) and she is pretty proud of it. She also seems quite proud of her outfit today.

We are going to a high school, and she is wearing Gucci. A tan Gucci belt is wrapped around her thin waist with a matching earth-toned brooch pinned to her collar. The rest of us are dressed casually in jeans and winter coats because Jamie told my mother that it was going to be a simple get-together with a kind tribute video and a short speech that he was going to deliver. My mother took that as a sophisticated event that required her rich widow outfit to be superb.

"Earth to Maggie!" Arlo snaps at me from across the table.

I can't seem to get out of my head recently. "Sorry; what happened?"

"Your mother just told everyone something important!" She hisses at me.

I look at my mother, and she cocks her head at me, "I was just saying that Jamie got some surprising news."

"What would that be?" I mumble, not caring.

"Leo didn't go home to care for a sick relative; she is leaving him."

I accidentally spit out my coffee on Reed's hand and cough harshly. Leo is leaving Jamie. She couldn't possibly be leaving him because of me, could she? It has been years since that happened and indeed if she knew then she would have left sooner...

"Maggie!" Reed yells, "What the hell?"

"I'm sorry!" I hand her some napkins and then look back at my mother, "Do you know what happened?"

She takes a sip of her Mimosa and grins, "He cheated! I don't know who she is, but I know she is younger than Leo and probably prettier! Donna from down the street told me Leo called to get the kid's transcripts from the school to transfer them before the break ended. She is moving in with her parents, and his cheating ass is all alone."

"Oh my God..."

I put my hand over my chest and feel myself start to panic. How is this happening? The whole town is going to find out what I did.

"Um, Mrs. Honors, Did Donna say who the other girl was?" Arlo asks.

Please tell me she didn't. Please tell me Leo did not tell the town gossip Donna Blanc that I slept with her husband when I was sixteen.

"Oh no, Leo didn't say who it was, but it happened more than once. Some idiot girl is going around thinking that he was going to leave his wife for her when in reality, he is just a selfish bastard."

"Maybe she never thought that! Maybe she was just lonely, and he caught her at a bad time! Maybe..."

Arlo stands up and interrupts me, "Maybe she should shut the hell up!" She pulls on my arm from across the table. I follow behind her as she begins to walk away.

We feel everyone's eyes on us but try not to look back at them. Can they see right through me?

Arlo pulls me into Taylor's room since it is the closest and then locks the door behind us. Running her fingers through her hair, she begins to groan. I have only seen her get mad at me like this once before- the Tom Holland incident.

It was six months ago, and I was working my regular shift at the coffee house right under our apartment. We were so busy I could hardly see at a certain point, but when I saw him it was clear as day. One of the internet's favorite white men asked me for a dirty chai for him and one of his friends. I knew what Arlo would give for a moment to be around him, and I also knew we had a blown-up magazine photograph of him framed in our living room. The coffee house was so busy, and I figured if I never told Arlo about it, then it would not matter. She would never have to know I didn't ask her celebrity crush for an autograph or a video of him saying her name over and over. So I decided to take his order and tell him to wait at the pickup counter for his chai's when they were done.

When I walked into my apartment several hours later, Arlo had gotten a villainous swivel chair in our living room and my favorite sweater in her right hand, along with scissors in her left. It turns out that the paparazzi had gotten pictures of me handing him his receipt through the window of the coffee shop. She was so angry that she cut right through my favorite sweater and turned the same shade of red as her hair. I swore never to make her that angry again. It looks as though I have now broken that promise.

"Just out of curiosity, what was the plan in there?" She asks me while grinding her teeth together.

I sit at Taylor's desk and cross my legs in his chair. The truth is that I am an idiot. If my mom knew the girl Leo was talking about was me, she would have killed me privately instead of airing out the town gossip at the breakfast table. "I just panicked."

"Look, I don't want to be the girl who says I told you not to have an affair with the creepy next-door neighbor or the girl that says I told you to tell your mom your creep next-door neighbor raped and groomed you, but I am going to be that girl right now."

"No way!" I yell a little too loudly, "The only reason I am freaking out right now is because we are home. The second that we go back to New York,"

"What?" She screams at me. "The second we go back to New York, this problem goes away? I have news for you, Maggie; the second we go back to New York, your dad is still going to be dead. The second we go back to New York, your family is still going to be a mess. The second we go back to New York, you are going to miss Ashton like crazy. The second we go back to New York, Jamie is still going to be the guy that stole something from you when you were young because, as I have previously stated, HE IS A PREDATOR!" She takes a moment to breathe before telling me in a much calmer tone, "We are getting a little too old for you to still be running away from your problems."

She opens the door and leaves Taylor's room, leaving me feeling like I am drowning in a pool of depression.

I need to talk to Jamie...

24

My old high school seems just as old and worn out as it did when I went here. In the theater hall (where I only went when Reed was in a play), there is still a giant hole in the wall that we used to refer to as "the void." Ryan Carter tried to put his arm through it once, but it reached nothing when he slid it through. I wonder if the teenagers attending school here respect the "please do not stick any body parts through the hole" sign Principal Hugo hung up.

Taylor and I walk past the tribute poster displayed in the lobby and laugh. "Loving father, neighbor, and friend."

"You know what is missing?" I ask him.

"Husband," He replies.

Despite their long-distance marriage, my parents never once spoke ill of their relationship in front of anyone. Well, anyone except for their children. My least favorite thing was when I was on the phone with my father in whatever city he was in at the time, listening to him go on about my mom not texting him back or calling him when she said she would and then having to listen to mom whine about how she has three kids to take care of. It was as though, Taylor, and Reed were these message carriers who got caught in the middle. Between a rock and another rock, Reed would say. I was not looking forward to hearing what my mom had to say about it.

"If we destroy the poster, then she never sees it and never complains about it..." He suggests only sounding half like he is joking.

I chuckle, "I think it is fine. It is not like this tribute was our idea. It was the towns. Maybe everyone realized they weren't happy."

"I think they were their version of happiness."

I rub his arm a little, "Keep in mind that is what you say about me."

"You're right," he whispers, "that is a terrible thing to say."

"Sometimes the truth is terrible, but that doesn't mean you don't say it."

He sighs a little, "It is also a terrible thing to speak with ill intentions and defend yourself by calling it the truth."

"What are you guys doing?" Arlo shouts at us from down the hall. "Your mom is about to go on stage!"

Taylor grabs my hand, and we run to the theater's double doors. Inside, many of the PTA members, teenagers from student government, and half of the nosey townspeople are sitting in their seats waiting to hear from the town's famous grieving widow. We take our seats in the front row and wait for our mother to begin her speech.

She takes a stand at the podium. Behind her are the faculty except one- Jamie. Jamie is the one who set up the whole thing, and he is also the president of activities here. I could take a shot in the dark why he is not here. Part of me wonders if Leo hated him for cheating or hated him for sleeping with a minor. Maybe she hated him for both. I know I did. Arlo slaps my arm, getting my attention just in time for my mother to begin.

"Hello, everyone! Most of you know who I am already, but if you do not- my name is Valentina Honors. My husband was the brilliant writer and producer Otis Honors to everyone, but to me, he was just Otis. He was the man I met on vacation with my parents years ago who had to ride a bike to his job at the Whataburger in Texas and, in his free time, liked to see movies early in the morning since they were five dollars. He was also the man that I raised three beautiful kids with."

I look down at my hands in an attempt not to roll my eyes. Her three beautiful kids she loved so much she didn't care to get to know.

"I remember the day we moved here. Maggie, my eldest, was still so little and hated moving out of our traveling bus. She threw such a big fit until Otis showed her how he decorated her room. He arrived here a week before we did so that he could decorate her room with her favorite books and a bed with a sleeping beauty comforter. I wondered at the time why he couldn't just wait until we all got here to do that but now, thinking back, I know it was because he was such a good person."

I remembered that comforter. Sleeping Beauty was and still is my favorite Disney movie. Dad got me her pink dress to wear, and I didn't stop wearing it for a year after. I had forgotten about it.

Tears fall elegantly down her cheek and land on her chest. Principal Hugo hands her a handkerchief that she takes without looking at him. "I..." she says, choking on her own words. "I think Otis did everything with our children in mind. He wrote for them. He traveled for them. He lived for them. And I know with my whole heart when he died, he thought of them."

Reed weeps with Taylor holding her as Ashton's hand grips my shoulder. I cry because my mother knows how to put on a show, but she doesn't know how to be honest about her feelings until she can't contain them anymore.

"Otis loved this town like you were a part of our family. He wanted you all to be okay even if he wasn't here anymore, just like he wanted for his children. I am so happy that he decided to donate more funding to help make lunches cheaper for those who need them; he wanted money to go to the art program so that your kids could do band and choir on top of science and math; he wanted the best for all of you because you wanted the best for him."

She bows toward the audience and then takes her seat next to Hughes. Her tears continue to fall, and my heart aches more for her now than it has this whole time. I feel her pain like never before.

"I miss him," Reed cries.

"I miss talking to him," Taylor says.

My chest starts to hurt. Sometimes the weight of your pain can feel like it is crushing but it could also mean you get so used to hiding how you feel that letting it out is scary. It could mean your body is so tired of you pretending that you're taking care of it but not doing anything. "I just miss knowing he was there," I say to them.

It shocks them to hear me say that. Hell... it shocks me too. There's something like being in Castine right now that I am eternally thankful for.

Taylor grabs my hand, and then Reed's, and we sit there just like that while lots of people take their turn speaking about our father, but none of them can beat the one and only Val Honors.

25

After everyone's speeches were done, and the tribute video played, we all convened in the cafeteria where my mom had catered from Cafe Aurora, which is the Italian restaurant down the road. Each table has a pretty light blue tablecloth with lily-covered place settings. My name is hand-written on a name placement where I sit next to Reed, Taylor, Mom, and Arlo. Ashton is at the house helping to make sure it is set for the photographer.

While today is a sorrowful day, it is also the day the photographer and journalist from Writers Envy come to the house to do their piece on my father. Mom laid out outfits for everyone to wear, including everyone from Arlo's family. Her dad's had some issues with the velvet suit jackets but other than that, they loved it. For me, she picked out a vest and pants combo. I like it fine, but it feels like something she would wear rather than me.

"How are you doing?" Arlo says knocking her shoulder against mine.

I lay my head on her shoulder and say, " I'm sorry about earlier."

"Me too. I know that I wasn't being very fair to you. It's just..." she takes a moment to breathe in and out, "you're not my best friend; you're my blood. I just want what is best for you, and I've been so worried these past few years that you don't want what is best for you. You want what you think you deserve and nothing more."

Wanting what I think I deserve and nothing more is the per-fect definition of who I am right now. "Do you remember when we were little and your dad had us do that exercise where we drew pictures of houses?"

"Yeah, you drew a black house with nothing on the outside and I drew my house with my dog and Ashton playing outside."

"Arlo..." I grab her hand and squeeze it three times, "I do not want to look at life that way anymore."

"I think the fact that you are saying that to me means you're starting not to."

I feel like I am about to cry again, but I try my hardest not to. The feeling of missing my father is beginning to drown me, but then again, I think it was supposed to all along. I look over to the dancefloor where my mom and Taylor are dancing to Adele's When We Were Young, which was one of my father's favorite songs. She seems to laugh at his jokes before he spins her around into the arms of Principal Hugo. He takes my mother's hand and dances with her elegantly, letting their feet glide against the floor to the same beat of Adele's music. There is this sense of wonder and curiosity about what they all might be talking about. If it were a different time, then I would assume they were talking about me and how disappointed they are in me, but I don't assume anything like that. I bet Taylor is telling Mom how beautiful she is, and Reed must have told him her suit was better than his. The two of them always fought about who looked better in some of the clothes they picked out. Principal Hughes favored Reed out of the three of us, so he probably picked her. I love the sight of them being happy. It makes me happy.

"What are you thinking about?" Arlo asks me.

"When I get to the end of the letters, I think I will be fine."

"Oh yeah? Even if it is not what you want to hear?"

I nod my head, "Yeah, I think what I want to hear is everything that could possibly make him not love me and I don't believe that he didn't love me anymore. I think he was just flawed, and everyone is flawed in some capacity."

She kisses the top of my head, "I think that is the most beautiful honest thing you have ever told me."

26

February 1, 2007
Dear Maggie,

My sweet Maggie, you are seven years old today. My baby girl is not so much a baby anymore. I like how each year that you get older and I write you one of these letters, you have no idea that I am doing it. One day I will give them to you and let you read each one. Perhaps something will surprise you. Maybe even shock you...

In all honesty, I feel as though I write these letters not for you but for myself. Having children is so terrifying because all you do is worry about your kids growing up too fast and not having enough time to be there for them. All I worry about is not having enough time with you. All I worry about is missing something.

Now that you are seven, you're different, which is not a bad thing. You usually love sitting down with me and reading, but lately, you've been doing that with Arlo. I miss making breakfast and sitting on the porch with all of you kids, smelling the clean air. Lately, you've been so busy with your homework and mom giving you chores so you don't rush to hang out with me in the morning or when you get back from school.

Today is different because you're off school, and it's your birthday. I got you a large bookshelf that David from the Hardwood store handmaid for you. Val and I are going to get some books with you today to put on it so you will have your choice of what books you are reading.

Your mom also made her famous German chocolate cake that you and I love. She has been busy all morning cooking and cleaning for you. It's amazing. All she asked me to do was stand by for my mom to call. Your mother adores me but my mother... let's just say she feels the same way about my mother as she does fermented beans.

I believe that is you walking down the stairs so before I leave you this, I will tell you that I love you my moon.

As always, today is my favorite day because it is your birthday.

Love Dad.

I decided to read my letter on my balcony today. If anyone came by I would just hide it under my blanket. I also noticed that I haven't read a book since I got home; probably because reading these letters is just like reading a novel.

My father was an excellent writer, even if that was difficult to admit sometimes. Going into a bookstore in Manhattan and seeing his very own table dedicated to his novels with all of the "now a major motion picture" stickers was like a punch to the face. It wasn't because I was jealous of him or anything. It had been years since I tried to write anything of my own that wasn't scripts for pilots that would never get picked up. There was just this feeling in my stomach like I couldn't escape him. I spent most of my childhood wanting him to notice me or be interested in who I was, so when I decided to leave my hometown and go to college with Arlo; I hated that I not only could never get away from him but that he didn't have to work hard to get away from me.

No one knew who I was. If they did, they knew me as his daughter. If anyone bothered to read anything I wrote it was followed with "You're Otis Honors daughter? Will he be helping you with this?" It was pure nepotism and nothing more that got me into any doors in New York, and I didn't want that. It wasn't right to use that. So I worked on my school assignments.

Anything I did was under my middle name Reynor. When I walked through those doors with that name- nothing happened. It always hurt, but at least it was the truth. He would never have to be haunted by the face of his daughter, whom he never cared for.

Now that I am getting to know this part of him, I feel guilty. He made mistakes all of the time as a parent, but don't all parents do? Is there truly one parent who has never made their child feel loved and supported at all times? Are there indeed children that can come into adulthood unscathed? Parents are just people of course and maybe it was easier to be mad at him than admit that he hurt me. It was easier to blame him than to talk to him about my feelings. Now I regret that more than anything. Looking back, he tried in different ways to connect to me and I just never let him get too close. The thought terrifies but it seems to be true that there was plenty of blame to go around when it came to my father, after all.

It is quiet in the house today. We spent the whole morning getting ready for the tribute and then being there for hours. Now that we were all home, everyone went to their separate rooms and slept. Arlo is passed out on my bed, and I am just on my porch with my dad's letters and a large white blanket. I look at Jayme's house and see through the window that most of the furniture is covered in white sheets... maybe he's moving?

Maybe he finally realized what we were to each other was wrong and losing his wife made him see that. Unfortunately, I know him too well to assume such a thing.

I go to get another letter when I get a text that distracts me.

Please come over. I need to talk. -Jamie

I know I shouldn't. I don't owe him anything at all but that doesn't stop me from feeling guilty. It doesn't stop me from wanting to apologize for her leaving. It doesn't stop me from telling him I'm on my way.

27

The walk from my house to Jamie's felt long. He's right next door, so it is not a long distance but I took my time. I slowly put on my shoes and then took each step down the stairs instead of just hopping down. I didn't tell anyone I was leaving. I just threw on my yoga pants and my gray zip-up and left.

I couldn't tell anyone I was leaving one because they were all napping but another reason was that I felt like it would be hard to explain. The man was just caught cheating on his wife who then proceeded to leave him. It would be difficult to tell them why I wanted to see him alone. This was frankly something that I just had to do.

Once I get to his house, I go around back through his gate, where the lock only takes a jiggle or two before it opens. I used to mess with this gate all of the time when we were sneaking around. I shudder at how familiar this is to me. The gate opens, and I shut it closed behind me. Jamie is waiting for me on his porch. It is cold but I have a feeling he doesn't care. Sometimes people just want to be numb.

I am unsure what to say so I don't speak at all. The silence is something I feel is necessary because if we talk and I apologize but he doesn't, I think I will cry, but if he apologizes and I don't, then I think I will still cry. The worst thing is that we both apologize and admit our faults and maybe, just maybe this thing that happened between us will not be an excuse for me to use anymore with Ashton or anyone. We will just become a thing of the past. A moot point in conversations about being a naive young girl; we will become nothing at all.

He grabs his drink from the table and then swallows it all as I still stand awkwardly in front of him. I am freezing, but I don't say anything. Instead, I just watch him. "It's far too cold; let's go inside." I take him up on his offer and follow him as he leads me to his living room, where the backdoor is still slightly broken from when I played soccer in the living room with his kids. "I am guessing the whole town must know by now."

"They don't know it was me if that is what you're asking." I sound bitter which is odd because that is not how I feel at all. Seeing his puffy blue eyes and hunched back over the counter, cradling his whiskey makes me feel... guilty. Is that even possible?

"Leo said she wouldn't tell anyone about that. She didn't want your reputation hurt by that. Mine, on the other hand- she just shredded it to pieces."

I sit at his kitchen island, playing with my fingernails like I usually do when I am nervous. Mom and Dad used to say they knew I was lying or hiding something when I bit my nails or tugged at my cuticles. "I am sorry she left you. I never wanted to hurt your family."

"You didn't," he says after taking another swig of whiskey, "I did. Not only did I cheat on my wife, but I also did it with our teenage babysitter. How fucked up is that?"

"Pretty fucked up," I tell him.

"Extremely," he agrees.

I rip my nail off my index finger and then ask him what I was never going to ask him, "Jaime, can you tell me why?"

"Why what?"

"Why did you sleep with me? Why did you want to?"

It is a question that I am not sure there is a perfect answer to, but I need to know how he answers it. There needs to be some reason from him that I never understood.

He pours more whiskey into his glass and slumps his shoulders. I think for a moment he is smiling, but I know that he is uncomfortable. He doesn't want to give me his answer which means it is the opposite of what I want to hear.

"I do not have an answer to make you feel any better."

I sigh, "I know that, but I need to hear you say it. I need the truth to come from your lips and not mine." I pleaded with him.

He takes a moment before taking a seat and then looks me dead in the eyes with no facade like he usually would, "I wanted to." I groan feeling frustrated because, to me, that is not an answer, but he goes on anyway. "I told you there is no answer that makes me a better person or makes you feel better. I am selfish, and I wanted you so I made it happen- that is that."

"You were right; you did not make me feel better."

I am about to get up and leave when Jamie's eyes go wide, and he seems frightened. When I turn around to see who he is looking at, I know why. My mother is standing behind us fuming with rage.

"Mom..."

She holds up her finger and walks past me abruptly. Jamie has never looked terrified in the entire time that I have known him, but he seems like he would jump out of a moving car over a bridge rather than be here right now.

"Val," Jamie starts but my mother cuts him off.

"Shut the fuck up right now," she hisses through her teeth. My arm starts to hurt and my chest starts pounding. This is the moment that I never wanted to see happen. My mother found out what I did, and what we did together, and knowing that there was nothing she could have done to stop it from happening because she didn't know. "You," she says, pointing her finger at Jamie like a knife, "You touched my daughter! When?"

"Jamie, don't," I warned him.

He doesn't hesitate, though "It was a long time ago when she was sixteen. I was twenty-three so it didn't feel wrong to me, I swear." She smacks him against his face so hard that he has to turn and hold his face from the pain seeping through his skin. What the fuck is happening? "I deserved that."

Her hands start shaking as she runs her fingers through her perfectly straight hair. I know her. I know when she is about to cry. "It didn't feel wrong? Is that why you hide it from your wife? Is that why you had her come over when Leo and the children were not home because it didn't feel wrong? You knew it was wrong!" She is screaming now making the pain in my chest get larger. It is the guilt coming for me now. I knew it would, I just didn't know when.

"I'm sorry," he says.

"Sorry? Do you think for a moment that sorry is enough? Do you think that you are even saying that to the right person?" He shakes his head no and her tears begin to fall. She gets closer to him and says, "You have no idea what little you will have once I am through with you!"

As she walks away she pulls at my arm dragging me along with her. We leave a horrified Jamie alone in his kitchen.

My anxiety gets even worse when I realize she just threatened to ruin him. Does that mean destroying me as well?

28

When Mom and I walked back into the house, she finally let my arm go and then ran upstairs. Taylor asked her if she was going to bed, and she yelled down, "Yes; however, do not come up here after me Taylor Honors!"

I went up to my room feeling Taylor and Reed follow me and thought if anyone was going to tell them it had to be me. Before the humdrum of the trophy wives down the street got their noses in this gossip. Before everyone would watch them as they went anywhere around town and whisper things as they walked by. I had to tell them my side of it as well as the other thing I was keeping from them- the letters. I wasn't finished with mine but I was sure by now that they did not include anything manipulative inside.

Once Reed shut the door, we all sat on my floor facing each other waiting for someone to speak first. I guess I had to just say something and then maybe the words would fall into place.

"Mom found something out just now that was upsetting and that is why we came home like that."

Reed tilts her head confused, "Maggie, the photographers that she has been waiting weeks for are almost here. What could have possibly been more important to her right now?"

Taylor rubs his forehead and says, "Maggie slept with Jamie Cartwright."

For me, it is the utter shock that makes me cover my mouth, but for Reed, it is amusement. I don't blame her for laughing because it sounds ridiculous when you hear it, but when Taylor and I say nothing, she understands that we are not kidding. It is not a silly prank, but something far more sinister and challenging to explain.

"Maggie," she says, "He is married."

"It gets worse," Taylor adds, "It started when she was six-teen."

"Okay, how do you know any of this?" I question him.

"Please don't hate me," he says as he sits up and leans on his palms. It worries me because he seems like he might cry but he also seems like he could kill someone. It is a look that only a woman with a brother would know. "When I was cleaning your room before you came, I found a diary in your trunk. I do not know what possessed me to read it, but once I did..."

"Would someone please fill in the sibling who doesn't like to violate people's privacy!" Reed screams at us.

I take a deep breath and then tell the story that I want to only think about when I listen to Taylor Swift's music on the subway to work. "I was very young, and back then, everything felt so final and bare when it came to this family and how we were. I was always alone, or at least it felt like it at the time. And Jamie was just there for me in a really awful way, but he was there at least."

"I don't understand..." Reed says, starting to tear up.

I grab her shoulder, "I never want you to understand. I never want you to feel like what I felt back then and then understand what I went through."

"We were there for you. We have always been there for you. You could have told me if he pressured you to have sex with him. I would have told Mom or Dad or someone, and I would have told you this is fucking creepy!"

My sweet Reed is far more potent than me and always has been. It is something I am eternally grateful for. "I know you would have. There is nothing I could say to cut myself some slack here."

She rolls her eyes, "You? Maggie, you were sixteen and he was twenty-three. You did not do anything."

"I knew that it was wrong."

That silences her. Taylor doesn't say anything, but he winces like I just threatened to hit him. Life, for everyone, is a novel. There are so many chapters, but if you skip or skim one, you are just confused. The other part of your story does not make sense. As much as I would like to, I cannot skip this chapter.

"My whole life you have been like this," Taylor says softly. "You never allow your feelings to be worth anything or mean something because you feel you are not allowed to have them, but you are. I understand that you knew it was wrong, but Jamie knew you were a child, and he was still attracted to you. You are allowed to feel violated and angry. You are allowed to feel anything that you want."

I know he is right. I always do this. I always make everything worse. If I feel too much then I am annoying and when I do not emote enough then I am a robot. There is little middle ground for people like me. There is only darkness.

Mother swings open the door and still looks frazzled but trying to keep herself together. "The magazine people are here. I need you all downstairs, and when they leave, we will have a family meeting with Maggie."

She slams the door shut leaving, sweeping wind through our hair.

Taylor helps Reed up from the ground but when he reaches for my hand I do not give it to him, "Can I just have a minute? I promise that I will be right down."

"Of course, you can."

They leave me alone after a moment of silence, and for the first time in the past few days, I feel like I used to feel when I sat in this room alone. I feel small. There is no joy or love or support, there is just this feeling of being small.

I cannot stay here. I cannot go downstairs and talk to this reporter and pose for these photos when my mother and siblings think of me as this horrible little girl who can't take care of herself.

Before I fully comprehend what I am doing, I grab my suitcase. I start throwing clothes into my bag and order a driver to the house. My chest gets that awful feeling like earlier when the anxiety inside of me is beginning to build up too much.

I get the alert that a driver is nearby and zip up my suitcase. I should leave a note or something so that no one thinks I was kidnapped or something. My shaky hand scribbles down; *I'm sorry, but I had to get away.*

The last thing that I grab from this room before climbing out of the window and running away like a child is the letters. My father's letters that he wrote for me have brought me great comfort in the time that I have been back home and in a way make me feel like that man I loved when I was a child was never gone; he was just lost. I try to ignore my thoughts about what he might think of me now if he found out about Jamie but luckily, that is the ugly truth he never has to come face to face with.

29

February 1, 2010
Dear Maggie,
*My sweet little moon, this is the year you hit the double digits in
life, as the kids say. Some things have changed, like how you do your
hair. You decided a few months back you do not like short hair anymore instead you want it long. The thing about that is you have such
thick hair and it grows so fast that it is already hitting the midpoint on
your back. You also decided that Arlo is the only person you consider
marrying. Arlo is like a daughter to me already, so that doesn't sound
like a horrible life for you. Some things have not changed, though. For
instance, you still like to be quiet with your feelings. You still hate it
when you do not get your way. The stickers on fruit get under your
skin and lastly, but most importantly, you are still your own person.*

*I worry that as a father, I have to watch things that I don't want to
see happen to my children, and something that deeply concerns me is
the need to fit in. You are only ten, so if you're reading this at forty and
this has happened to you, know that it is okay. I just like that you take
a book wherever you go even if it is to a party at school. I love how you
laugh at things that no one else thinks are funny. I love that when you
go to Taylor's games you scream so loud he can hear you on the track. I
just love you.*

*I love the person that you are becoming. I love that as each year
goes by my sweet little girl becomes more and more of a force to be
reckoned with.*

As always, I love you very much, baby. Happy birthday!
Dad

The plane ride is the perfect place to tear through some of my letters. It is also a great distraction from my phone. If I am reading this then I won't check my phone to see everyone has realized that I am gone. My father is known for his captivating words, and at a time like this- his talent is needed.

Now that I am away from everyone again; I can breathe. I felt so surrounded and anxious not that running away like a child fixes anything, but it sure does buy me some time to deal with it. The matter of Arlo is something different. The second she finds out I ran out, she will be on the next flight out to yell at me so I have to get myself together before that happens.

"Can I ask what you are reading?" The elderly lady next to me asks.

"Um, these are some letters my father wrote me when I was little."

She smiles at me, "Forgive me for being so nosey dear. I think it is fascinating to see a young woman with letters. Most people your age do not care for those anymore just texting this and video calls that."

"Honestly, I didn't know I would love reading them, but I do. I haven't been able to think about much else."

"How old is your father?" It is the first time that I am saying it to a stranger and the thing is that I feel broken. It was how I was supposed to feel when I heard the news and when I arrived home but I didn't. This woman with her sunflower hat and pink ladies' shift on will forever be known as the woman who made me cry on the airplane in front of strangers. "Darling? Is everything okay?" Her hands rub my shoulders as the tears keep coming with no intention of stopping. It is a great comfort having her here with me. Having someone who doesn't know and is not judging me and letting me cry over my father is excellent. I feel liberated in a way.

"I'm sorry..." I say trying to wipe my tears away, "My dad, he um, well he died not too long ago. I was here visiting with my family for his funeral and tributes."

"Oh, my big mouth. It has always been a problem. I am so sorry for your loss honey."

"It's okay. I do not think it sunk in until right now that he's gone."

"My dad passed away when I was itty bitty. It was an awful feeling like a part of me was missing but my mom told me something that helped me. Parents are meant to die before their children, and children live on with their memory keeping them alive."

She is a sweet woman comforting a strange girl crying on a plane. She is also suitable. My dad is gone, and I wish I had not been so prideful and angry. I wish I had more time to get to know him without hovering in this bitterness that he was not there for me as much as I wanted him to be.

"I was so cruel to him when he was alive. I wish I could tell him I loved him now."

Her hands grip my face, shaking slightly but bringing warmth to me nonetheless. "He knows you loved him. As a parent myself, I can promise you this."

"Thank you."

The man sitting on the other side of her starts weeping which makes me laugh, "That is beautiful."

"I know honey," she says, comforting him, "I have always been good with words."

I feel sleepy and ask them to wake me when we get close to landing. My head slumps over my shoulder and rests against the window, and I allow myself to drift off without worrying about anything else going on in my life.

30

My apartment is a closet. We have a one-bedroom that we turned into two bedrooms by converting the dining room to my room and a small area where our kitchen is, but we consider it a hallway. If Arlo and I wanted to make food at the same time, we would have to wait for the other one to be done before going in. While it is minimal in space, I missed it. My home away from my childhood home. My neighbors sell weed to elderly people for medical conditions, and the coffee across the street is only four dollars if you want something other than drip at your house.

My key turns the lock and an empty apartment awaits me when I open it. I crave solitude, and being surrounded by family for days was a bit hectic. Even when Arlo is home, she is rarely inside the apartment. The frat boy likes to take her out to plays and expensive Italian restaurants his parents have ownership in. I don't date myself so it is usually just me here.

I throw my bags on the ground and pull out my phone again, expecting to see something, but there is nothing. No angry text messages or several dozen calls from Arlo and Taylor. Perhaps they are freezing me out. It is fully possible, considering I just ran away from everyone including Ashton. He was working on the house for us while we were at the tribute, and I told him I would meet him after the photographer but I didn't. Instead, I got the whole family pissed about Jamie and I before the magazine staff even got there.

I cannot sulk about this. I need food and sleep. I pull out my iPad and open my food delivery app. My inability to cook anything makes my points on apps like these astounding. As I find my favorite spring roll restaurant, the doorknob turns.

Considering Arlo and I live here alone, no one should have a key. Panicking, I pick up a pillow ready to throw it at whoever comes in.

the door fully opens and Arlo appears. She sees my defense pillow and laughs, "Mags, we have lived in New York for years. Surely you know that a pillow would do nothing to a prospective rapist."

"What the hell are you doing here? I thought you were in Castine still."

"I was, but when you didn't come out of your room, Taylor asked me to check in on you and I found your note."

"Oh," is all I can think to say.

She sets her bags down on the ground next to mine and then takes a seat on our ottoman. "I got the flight out right after you which I know is disappointing considering you ran away hoping to mope alone."

"I would much rather mope around with you. "

"Maggie, why did you run away?"

Because I am an idiot who cannot emote healthily. "My mom was screaming about how she was going to ruin Jamie, Taylor was mad at me for not being mad at Jamie and Reed was just... disappointed in me. She has never been disappointed in me because she's Reed but when she looked at me, it was like she had never been so upset with me I didn't know what to do. "

"You are so fucking dense sometimes."

I hug my pillow for comfort, "I know, I fucked up everything."

"Not because of that! Because your family was in so much pain learning you had been taken advantage of and you somehow turned that into them being angry with you!"

"They were angry!"

She shakes her head, making her red hair swing back and forth on her face. "They were angry at him! They were not angry at you! Do you think I have ever blamed you for what the two of you did? Do you think Ashton did? No! You were taken advantage of because you were vulnerable to your feelings. You have never allowed yourself to fully feel something because if you do, you might figure something out about yourself that you hate. Guess what? Everyone feels like that! Everyone is worried that they are too much."

"I don't know what you want me to say here."

"It is not about what I want you to say! It is about what you want to say! How do you feel about Jamie? How do you feel about your dad? How do you feel that you are now the owner of a major publishing company?"

"I am pissed off! I am fucking angry all of the time; is that what you want from me?"

She diminishes the space between us and then grabs my shoulders, "Why are you angry?"

The feeling in my chest where I feel like I might collapse begins except this time, I release myself from it. "I am mad because I had a stupid crush on a neighbor but I was in love with your brother and instead of losing my virginity to him- I lost it to someone who took it from me without asking me if I wanted him to. I am mad because my whole life my mother taught me to be perfect and hide my feelings, but wanted me to tell her about Jamie anyway. I am mad because my father, the one person who saw me for who I was, was never around! I am mad because I hate my fucking life!"

I took a moment to catch my breath, but Arlo got what she wanted from me. She finally got me to say all the things out loud I swore to keep to myself. She seems pleased though her smile has appeared again.

"That," she says, kissing my forehead. "Is exactly how I thought that would go."

"What am I supposed to do now?"

"Take a day to sort out your shit, and then we are the first flight back to Castine to make it right with everyone."

I roll my eyes, but not at her, at myself for the mess I must have made. "How bad is it back home?"

"Well, your new relationship with Ashton is on the rocks, if I am being honest."

Shit! I knew he would be pissed at me. His lack of blowing up my phone is telling. "Excellent," I say sarcastically.

31

An old saying in my family is "Do not bite the head off of the messenger- bite the head off of your feelings." I used to think that meant keeping your feelings buried inside yourself, but I am not so sure anymore. In each letter I read, as I got older, my father seemed worried about me not letting myself grow into an adult who felt like my feelings were valid. I think that old family saying was trying to tell me to rip open my feelings and let them make themselves known even if it is hard and even when it makes life difficult because if I don't then I could explode.

There are 22 letters from my father, each written on my past birthdays, and 12 of them have brought me back to life. They are complicated, unique, and enticing. The words fly off of the paper and into my heart the same way I dreamed as a little girl, he would talk to me in person. I wish he was still here, still just a phone call away, so I could ask him how to fix the mess I made.

I am on my bed at the moment, holding the envelope for letter thirteen, wanting to devour

each letter until I get to the end, but I realized about thirty minutes ago when Arlo said she would be getting dinner for us from Pizza Palace that the more I read the closer I am to the end. The closer I am to not having him with me anymore. There was a huge part of me that worried I couldn't mourn a father I didn't know, but I know now that I have always known him because he and I are one. Two people obsessed with time, but not the people in our lives. He spent most of his life loving me with his words on pieces of paper instead of to my face because he wanted me to have a good life. He worked endlessly, most likely working himself to death, because he thought that was what mattered, and I do not want to live my life like that. I want to work, fall in love, travel, be with my family, and know that when I leave this life I do not regret anything. I want to die when I am old knowing my life felt full until the very end.

I hear the door to our apartment open and wait for Arlo to find me contemplating life in my unicorn party t-shirt that I got when I went to a gas station on a field trip in high school. It is not an outfit for a mature young woman. Luckily, I am not a mature young woman yet.

I call out for her. When she does not come into my room with the food, I yell out, "Arlo, can you please just bring me the pizza? I am depressed about my life choices at the moment."

"Wow, I guess I am a disappointment." I jumped up, frightened at the sight of him, not because I did not want him here, but because I did not think I would be seeing him. Ashton, my Ashton, is standing at my door fresh from the airport with his bag hung over his shoulder. He puts his bag on my desk chair and then shoves his hands in his pockets. "I had this whole romantic gesture planned out, but then I thought maybe you didn't want the romantic gesture, so I got nervous and cried on the cab ride here, and now I am not sure what I should say."

I do not know why the first thing I can think of to say to him is, "I got this shirt a long time ago."

He laughs at me, "I know. I was there when we all went to Salem."

I look at his whole body and, it is stunning- he is gorgeous like always. He is wearing that black leather jacket that Arlo got him for Christmas a few years back that I love and his Italian boots I got him from the thrift store in Castine when I was eighteen. It is an excellent and sexy combination which makes it difficult to focus on what I want to say. I was a bitch for running away, and forgive me.

I cough, trying to clear my throat from choking on my nerves and try to say something to explain myself. "Ash, I left... it was not because of you. I just got overwhelmed by it all."

He nods, "I knew it was not because of me. You have a lot going on, and the plan was to give you some space."

"And that is why you came here? You flew to New York so that you could give me space?" It is adorable that he is here. He is the perfect example of someone being adorable.

"I decided that space was stupid when you are in love, so I came here."

He doesn't notice that he said it right away, but I do. My heart started beating fast, and my palms got sweaty but in a good way, In the way that you feel like anything could happen, and it was so exciting that you had these new possibilities presented to you. I had Ashton flying to New York to tell me that he loved me and that, it was the definition of true love.

The second he realizes that he said it, his eyes go wide, and I worry he might regret saying it, so I run up and jump onto him, wrapping my legs around his waist. "I love you too," I whisper into his ear.

"Oh, thank God," he says, squeezing my waist and kissing my neck, "that was almost really embarrassing," He holds me like this for a minute before kissing me. It is quick, beautiful, and also the best kiss I have ever had.

"Can I reveal myself yet?" Taylor appears out of nowhere and surprises more than Ashton did just a few moments ago.

"Taylor! What are you doing here?"

Ashton sets me down but still keeps an arm around my waist. "You're my big sister, and you disappeared without notice. Did you think I was not going to come after you?"

Taylor, my protector, is back and better than ever. He seems tired, with his eyes lacking life in them and his cheeks puffy. I'm sure running out on everyone was awful and confusing. For Taylor, he can take that as a sign that I need him to comfort me, but for Reed and Mom... "Mom and Reed are in the living room, then?"

He looks down at the ground avoiding eye contact while telling me the truth, "Maggie, they just take things personally, you know that."

"So, did Reed curse me once or twice?"

Ashton throws his hand over his mouth, and Taylor smiles, "Only three times," Taylor replies.

"Look," Ashton says, pulling on my arm and making me face him, "We came here because you have to face this. You love your family, and you love Castine, and you want Honors Publishing more than anything; you just are afraid to admit you want all of that."

"We don't want you to run away anymore," Taylor adds, "We would like it if you ran towards us."

"Is this some sort of love intervention?" I ask them.

"Yes!" They shout simultaneously.

I pull them into a hug and feel myself give in without worrying about anything else. My life and my happiness is with my family. I also realize that it has been long enough. The letters need to come out to everyone, especially my family.

"Taylor?" I say into his chest.

"Yeah?"

"I have something I need to tell you."

32

February 1, 2022

My love, today is my favorite day- your birthday. This is the year you graduate, and I decided the best thing to get you is something that could inspire you to come home to me and your mom. I got a car that can fit all of your stuff in that closet you call an apartment in New York and my new book inspired by you. My main character is someone that I wanted to feel closer to, and the one person that I have not felt close to in the past couple of years is you.

You have your own life where you go to school and have multiple jobs in New York to make ends meet, so I get that you do not want your old dad cramping your style or anything, but I miss you. I thought that maybe if I gave you the idea to come home, you would. Your mom wanted you to have a diamond necklace and ship it to your apartment, but I know you would roll your eyes at it. You are not like your mother with that stuff. She loves diamonds and clothes, but you are like me because you want to feel something. You want to find meaning in life just like me.

There is something else that I want you to have and something difficult for me to hand down to you. I want you to have Honors Publishing when you graduate. I know what you are thinking; Dad, you are insane! Hear me out; when you graduate, you will learn under me for a year, and then I will pass down the company to you and retire. My life has been filled with everything that I could want. I have a beautiful wife, a big house, three children, and a career where I have done everything I hoped I would. It is time for me to move on.

I want the rest of my days to be about being a dad, and hopefully, being a grandfather someday (no rush on that). If I am still traveling, then I could miss seeing you guys becoming the best people the world has to offer. It would be nice to have you in Maine at least. New York is overrated if you ask me.

There is no one I would trust with this other than you.

As always, I love you, baby girl.
Dad.

Arlo is chewing on her pizza on my floor while Taylor looks into the abyss of my father's last letter to me. It is shocking to read something from someone who is not with us anymore. His face reminds me of when I found the letters in his study.

"I do not understand this. There are 22 letters from him here. I only read some of them with you. How is it possible that you hid them from me?"

"I just wanted to protect you guys! What if these letters were just a bunch of manipulative lies about him being the best dad, and it was our fault he was not around?"

Taylor rolls his eyes at me, and when I look to Arlo for help, she shrugs her shoulders and eats her pizza.

"Do we all get them, or is it just you?" He asked me.

"There were three stacks of letters each with our names on it, so each of us will get them."

"Why didn't he give us these when he was alive?"

"I don't know. I think he thought they were these photo albums and one day he would give them to us, but he didn't have time to. He sounded like he would have given them to us eventually."

Taylor sighs and falls over onto my bed. It is a lot to take in. We lost our father a short time ago, and what I felt towards him my whole life versus now is fundamentally different. Taylor, on the other hand, always loved my parents and never held a grudge against them. He wanted to; that much was obvious, but he didn't because they were our parents, and having anything against them was a waste of time. He would always tell me that they were our parents when I wanted to complain about them. We didn't get a spare set when we didn't like our first pair. These letters gave me some peace when it came to how I felt about them, but I never considered it would only make Taylor confused by their existence. He lived with Mom and Dad as well as Reed. They ate dinner together and went on trips together. There was no confusion about where they stood until this moment.

"My whole life, I wanted him to talk to me like this in person, and he never did. What if my letters are not like yours? What if he only wanted to write these personal letters to you? Reed and I would get the pity letters he wrote out of duty."

I get how he could question Dad's intention with these letters because I did. It did not make sense how he could show us one thing and do the other until I fully read them, and when I look back at my life with him; I know that it was because I didn't bother to look at him enough that I didn't see how much he truly loved me.

"Taylor, he loved you more than anything."

"I know that makes sense in my head, but..."

I cut him off before he could say anything else, "I'm not sure why he did some of the things that he did, but I know with all my heart he loved us so much. I know that is why he worked so hard so that we would never have to worry about not paying for college or having to work jobs in high school to help him pay rent. I know that even when Mom was difficult, she was still the person he fell in love with and had three kids with. I know after everything that I have read and thought about that we all meant the world to him." Taylor squeezes my hand, and a small tear falls down his cheek. "Parents are not perfect, they are just people who had kids, and now they have to figure it all out."

"I love you, Maggie," Taylor says.

"I love you too."

It is silent for a minute, with only the sound of Arlo and Ashton eating pizza in the corner filling the space in my room. Finally, Taylor sits up with his tears coming at a slower pace and his smile back once more. "I'm going to sleep on your couch, and when will all get up in the morning and go back to Castine as a group, get Reed to undo her curses on you, and then tell her and mom about the letters. Maybe after all of that, someone will be kind enough to get me a chocolate croissant from the bakery because I have had a hard week!"

He storms out with Arlo deciding to follow him. Ashton and I are left alone in my room, and I feel the exciting pull toward him.

"Am I allowed to sleep in here?" He asked me.

"Sleep? You can stay here but not for that."

He smiles and makes his way to my bed. Sitting on his knees, he parts my own and whispers against my thigh, "I can make some arrangements..."

33

I wake in the morning to Ashton wrapped around me, his breath warming my neck. He's still naked from the night before, as am I, and he's got this adorable smile permanently etched onto his face. Maybe in the future, we could have more mornings just like this together.

His chin starts to rub against my neck, and his hand caresses my thigh. "This bed is far too small."

He is right. I bought the twin bed with the thought that no one but me would be in it. I only had one person in here that I was dating, and Blue thought that my Vinyl collection was a disappointment, so they went home early. Ashton is someone I want in my bed at all times if I can have it. I turn around to face him and his deep brown eyes pull me in just like they did last night. He smells so rich in vanilla and oils, making me breathe him in. "I would like a bigger one, but I am afraid my room would have even less space."

"My bed fits us both with no problem."

"I have not been in your bed."

"Yes, you have! We used to have sleepovers all of the time."

I run my fingers through his hair, and those beautiful curls I love so much just slide through my fingers. "Ash, I was thirteen the last time we did that. I am twenty-two now."

"You are never too old for sleepovers, Maggie."

I bring my lips up to his, and we get caught in the same cycle we did last night. Kissing, rubbing, thrusting, and all of it combined is enough to end me. Things are about to move forward when my door swings open with Arlo in her robe and green tea face masks startling us.

"Ew! Can you guys not do this when I am home?" She shrieks.

Ashton sits up and groans, "Lo, we are adults; by now, you would know to knock on the damn door."

"Whatever, move over," she moves Ashton's legs to make some space for herself to sit, "We need to set some ground rules here." Neither of us says anything to her, so she continues. "I am happy for the two of you; however, I need some help adjusting to this, so no overly affectionate displays of affection. I need not hear you two call each other by cute nicknames. The most important rule here is that you understand that I need to be the most important person in both of your lives."

"Deal," we say together.

"Excellent! Now you guys need to get up! We have a plane to Castine to catch."

Arlo and I sent emails to all of our professors explaining the family emergency was taking a few days to handle because we were supposed to be back at school tomorrow, and we will not be. Luckily, all of them understood and gave us makeup assignments. I am about to graduate soon, so I want to be on my A game; I also need to sort things out with my family, or my head might explode.

When we all arrived in Maine, I felt like I was having deja vu. It was only over a week ago that Arlo and I were rushing to get to my dad's funeral on time, and now we were all heading to Castine together to fix my mess with my family. I also had a boyfriend which is not the most crucial detail, but one I like to keep telling myself.

I have a boyfriend.

Ashton is my boyfriend.

Yes, it still sounds perfect.

34

"Are you going to open the door?" Taylor whispers into my ear.

I thought that at least getting through the door would be a simple task, but alas, it is not. The truth is that as much as I want to clear the air with my entire family, I also want to keep things foggy. Once everything is said, it cannot be unsaid. There is no taking anything back once the can of worms unleashes itself. My hand grips the key in my hand, and despite everything inside of me that tells me now is the time to run- I don't run. Instead, I turn the key and open the door to my childhood home with Taylor behind me. "Let's go."

We throw our bags on the ground and look around, expecting Mom and Reed to be in the living room, but to our surprise, they are not. I worry for a moment that there will be some silent treatment from the two of them, but once Taylor yells for both of them, they scream back that they are in the dining room.

"Mom, I am sorry..." I stop dead in my tracks when I see the changes or I guess, the changes back. Our dining room table is back, along with many cookbooks, and the beverage cart from my grandmother. The painting that Reed did is back on the wall, and my father's favorite flower, the Iris, is in the middle of the table, made into a centerpiece. The smell of chocolate mint chip cookies, our family's favorite, and red velvet cookies, my favorite, are on plates on the table. The smell is intoxicating, not to mention distracting. "What happened here?"

"I always planned on putting everything back once the magazine staff was done meddling about my house." She takes a sip of her coffee, but something seems off with her. It is something about the way she is calm that is terrifying. Almost as if she was planning my demise at this very moment. She gestures toward the chair across from her, and I take a seat waiting to be scolded. "Do you kids remember how I used to think having family meetings over cookies every week was necessary?"

"Yes, but we do not need to do that anymore," Reed argues.

Mother grins and then leans back into her chair. "I thought so too, I was wrong. So, we are going, to be honest with each other about absolutely everything starting with Margaret."

She full-named me. She means business. "Okay, where do I start?"

"Start with Jamie!" Reed begs.

"Okay," I reach for some tea in the middle of the table and try not to smile when I realize my mother has put out my favorite breakfast tea. Maybe she is not mad at me after all? "It started when I was sixteen, and it was a mistake. I ended things when I went to college." There is not a good way for me to phrase that which makes sense to anyone, but there it is. A giant mistake on my part that I would take back if I could.

"I will go next," Taylor says, "Maggie did not use your credit card in Hartford to buy makeup when we were fifteen, Mom, I did."

"I knew that but thank you," Mom says.

"You still grounded me?" I practically screamed, "Even though you knew Taylor did!" I got a whole week's worth of errands and her endlessly ranting about money for that one!

She shakes her head, "He did it, and you lied, so if you want to take on the responsibility, then you get to take on the punishment too." Her ways of parenting have always been interesting. Dad simply made me write a paper on the value of money and then lit it on fire in the fireplace. "Now, who wants to go next?"

"I will go," Reed answers. "Mom, I like girls."

Mom rolls her eyes and grabs a mint chocolate chip cookie, "It is not sharing if it is something that we already know."

"I have something else to tell everyone." It is now or never with these secret letters, so I reach for my purse on the floor and pull them out. Spreading them out on the table, I feel the urge to vomit. These are not just for me anymore. They have to be for everyone, and there is a sickening feeling that comes with that thought. I feel as though I have had my dad all to myself, and I know that I will miss that.

Reed starts looking through the letters, skimming through them before handing them back to me. My mother, on the other hand, seems unraveled. She doesn't even look at the letters. All she does is keep her eyes on me, reading me, just like she did when I was younger, and she could tell I was lying. "Mother," I say with my tone sharp as ever, "Why do you look like you have seen these before?"

"Of course, I have seen them before," she says with a monotone voice, "I am the one who put them in that drawer after he passed away."

The words I want to say do not seem to come out of my mouth. I try, even begging my inner monologue, to ask her all kinds of things, but nothing happens. Our eyes are locked on each other, and the more that I look at her, the more things start to make sense. The note that I found was, Maggie, open your letters first, someone had to write that and why would it matter to Dad who opened their letters first? The answer is that it wouldn't. My mother knows me as the skeptic and cynical, but also the one my siblings follow behind. She needed me to open my letters first to understand what they were and then pass the message along to the others. "How I didn't see that is beyond me."

"Why didn't you give us all the letters when he died?" Taylor asked her with just a hint of exasperation.

She sighs while flipping her perfect hair over her shoulder. After taking a moment, she explains. "I loved your father since I was a teenager, and because I have loved him for so long, I knew him better than anyone. I knew why he felt like he had to be out of town all of the time and why he felt like having his writing career and businesses were essential, but there were times when we would argue over what kinds of parents we wanted to be and our views did not always align. I knew he had begun writing the letters when Maggie was born, and I just thought that if she read hers first and understood what they were and how much he loved you, all of you, more than anything, maybe they would feel more sincere."

Sincere. It was an interesting word to describe how a series of letters could make me feel loved by a man I thought did not care for me since I was a child. "I thought he hated me..."

Her hands pull on mine, making me look at her again. This time when we make eye contact, barriers feel knocked down. The rare moment when she is not trying to be perfect and instead just tries to be a mother is back. "He adored you. He adored all of you! This is something that all of you will find out someday when you have your kids, but being a parent is the hardest thing in the world. You have no control over how your kids see you, even when you try your best to be the perfect parent. All that you can do is love them and hope that is enough. All I ever wanted in this world was to have children and watch them grow up to be these amazing people, and it breaks my heart that your dad's time with you guys was cut short."

I am not sure what overcomes us, but we all get up from our seats and surround our mother. Each of us gives her a big hug while she cries softly, ruining the makeup that she worked so hard on when she got up in the morning. As each of her mascara-infused tears fall, so do my walls with my family.

I am on the couch in my living room reading when my mother finds me again. After our talk earlier, everyone parted ways to help clean up the house, and get some alone time. Honors do not emote well, and that was the most emotional conversation we ever had as a family. It has been a couple of hours since anyone has acknowledged me, but she appears from the dining room and takes a seat next to me.

"Hi, my child."

"Hi, Mom," I gave her my blanket because it was freezing in the living room just like usual.

She moves her feet under it and then starts to rub my leg. "I came to check on you. I know you do not like to be open with us."

It irritates me how much she knows me. "I'm fine. I was going to tell you that I decided to take on Honors publishing once I graduate from school."

She smiles like she is proud but refuses to say it. "What made you change your mind?"

If I am being honest, I do not think I was ever going to say no. I was confused as to why he would leave me something so unique to him and personal when he never seemed to understand who I was as a person, but I was wrong. "I think I finally felt connected to him and you for the first time in my life, and Honors Publishing feels like it is mine. It feels like it is my calling."

"I am so glad to hear that." She pulls me into a deep hug. I feel her play with my hair tossing it out of the messy ponytail I had it in before. When she pulls away, she kisses my forehead and then stands up to leave. "Before I go," she says, pulling an envelope out of her pocket, "There was one more letter written for each of you to read. Taylor and Reed just read it, so it is your turn."

She places the envelope in my hands, and I take the letter out of the off-white envelope that has aged, just like all of his other letters. I lean back on the couch and read...

October 13, 2006
Dear children,

Maggie, Taylor, and Reed, if you are reading this, then that means that your mother thought you needed it after my unfortunate passing. Hopefully, this letter does not find the three of you until I am so old that I yell at the neighbor kids for messing with my grass (even though I do not necessarily care if they do), and if you are reading this sooner than I had expected, I am so sorry. Parents are meant to die before their children. No one likes it, but that is the natural order of things. I do hope, more than anything, that you all have extraordinary lives. I imagine Maggie being a successful writer married to a handsome Greek guy she met while traveling. Taylor, in my head, you are this adorable dorky dad living in our house, happily married with multiple children. Reed, my little unicorn, I know you are traveling the world, meeting different kinds of people, and loving your life doing whatever it is you decided to do for the rest of your life. Each of you is happy in your life, but you thrive when you get together, just like when you were kids. Everyone comes home to Castine, where you all grew up, to celebrate holidays and momentous occasions. Maggie remembered to buy your mother lilies for Christmas morning just like I always did. Your kids grow up to be the best of friends because their parents are not only siblings, but they are also the famous Honors trio. I know that I am working hard to give you all a good life where money is not an issue, but what I want you to understand and grasp is that your kids are the loves of my life. I wake up in the morning for you. I work hard for you. I dressed up like a fairy and drank pretend tea for you. I helped your mother glue rhinestones to a shirt for Reed's first birthday. I watched all of the Barbie movies with Maggie. I do nothing in my life anymore without thinking of the three of you. Maybe I didn't do it the best way, or perhaps I did. Maybe I left too soon or when I was crippled with a cane. What I do know with everything inside of me is that while I may leave you with a house, cars, money, or a company; what I need you to do is please remember I left you each other...

All of my love,
Dad.

I close the letter and stick it back in the envelope. "I promise I will remember that for the rest of my life Dad," I say to myself. I look over my shoulder to a picture of the three of us with Dad when we visited Texas in Tyler swimming. My thumb rubs the picture of him bright and happy with his arms slumped over all of our shoulders.

My memory of my father is no longer tainted, instead, it is sacred.

Sometime in the future

Dear Otis,

After nine months of bodily agony and 21 hours of labor, you are finally in this world with us. I am a Mother, thanks to you. I have to admit that I was nervous about meeting you today. There have been several occasions when I have made a wrong first impression, but I think that I nailed it.

The moment that you came out of me, the doctors handed you to me and placed you on top of my chest. I felt your tiny little heart settle once it met my own and your screams disappeared. Your father was worried you might be uncomfortable at first because you kept on squirming around on top of me but I know you better than he does already. Ashton thinks he is going to make you love him more than me but that seems impossible to me. You are my favorite person in the whole world and I am sure that as you get older you are going to remind me that is true all of the time.

Your uncle Taylor is currently with you in the newborn wing. He just got out of school and is doing his residency here so when I told him I picked this hospital to have you he practically shrieked. He is thrilled to be an uncle and I suspect that his new girlfriend Kate is going to be the one to have beautiful babies with in the future. She has been so great taking care of me since you living inside of me also meant that it was difficult to do daily tasks like getting out of bed without looking like I am a turtle on my back. Your Aunt Reed is on her way back now from Italy and is sending me a text every ten minutes to see if there is anything new with you. I don't have the heart to tell her that you are a newborn and the only thing you want to do is sleep. When she gets here, she might be your favorite. Reed, as you will soon find out, is her own kind of person which means she is everyone's favorite. Your newborn hat that is blue with the little OH stitched into it she handmade even though I did not tell her your name yet.

You having your dad's last name is a given but the rest of it was mine for the picking. Otis Honors, you are not the first with that name but you are my firstborn. I wanted you to have your grandfather's name for a multitude of reasons but the biggest being that the second I got pregnant with you I started to have dreams where he was visiting me again. It had not happened since he passed away but I like to think that he knew you were coming and wanted to remind me of something he taught me a long time ago. I am going to love you as fiercely as possible because you are my everything. I love you more than anyone that I know. I will fight for your happiness over my own at any point that comes up. I will give you anything you need and help you get anywhere you want. You, my little Otis, are the definition of perfection, and do not let anyone tell you otherwise.

Your life is going to be filled with some interesting relatives. Surely the ten minutes you spent with Grandma when she told you that you could have been named Valentino showed you that but you also need to understand that our family is extremely close. You will never grow up feeling alone or unloved because you have the best people around. I promise you from now on that no matter where life might take us, our family will always show up for you.

Until next year my little moon,
XOXO Mom.

The Castine Ledger

A day with Leona Lake
A local favorite and soon to be TV show creator.

Our lead journalist, Lloyd Jacob was able to set up a one on one with soon to be famous television creator Leona Lake (formally Leona Cartwright) about the inspiration for her new show The Father. Leona sold the rights to the show after it was pitched in LA last March and found herself drowning in offers after admitting the inspiration for the show came from secrets in her own marriage.

Below is the transcript from that conversation.

Interviewer: Did you find it difficult to make something out of your past marriage?

Leona: Not really. There was a lot of built up rage and resentment leftover. Creating this show was a way to let it out and grieve.

Interviewer: Greif with a relationship is always difficult. Usually, you see couples fighting over houses, kids, reputations, but your ex-husband, Jamie Cartwright, has not fought you on anything. You two sold the house amicably. You have full-custody of your kids. He refuses to comment about the show. How did you manage to get him to be so civil with all of this? If I wrote a television show about how awful my ex-wife was, then she would have me by my throat for my assets.

-

Leona: I have found when your ex-husband has a plethora of secrets he has kept from you and one day you stumble on all of them, he tends to be more inclined to compromise on most things. It is better for him for me not to write a television show about everything I know than just the one thing.

-

Interviewer: The show is based on your marriage to him and the affair that ended everything for you two. It makes me wonder what you could have possibly left out for his sake...

-

Leona: As long as he does what he is told and stays out of my town (Castine), then you and the world will never know.

Acknowledgments

When I write a book, the first thing that comes to my head is, "Will someone find joy in this?" This was the first time that I didn't ask myself that. This book was more of a way to let myself explore the relationships in life that do not get romanticized enough. The love from a family is a powerful one. Growing up, I thought that everyone hated me including my own mother but each year that I get older, I understand that is not true. Families are not meant to be perfect. They are not meant to be fully functional at all times and no matter how wild my family is they are my everything. I wanted to take the time to honor that love in my heart for them as well as let them know that no one is the perfect least of all parents. Sometimes we can judge the ones we love under a microscope without allowing imperfections. This was my way of giving my family and maybe yours the feeling that we can sometimes take for granted; family, whatever that looks like to you, is always there for you no matter where you end up in life.

About the author

Michaela Ryanne is a self-published author from Texas. She got her start writing on Wattpad before graduating her first novel from the screen to the page. Her favorite genre of books is romance which is also her favorite thing to write. She spends her free time reading and playing with her dog at home.

A Special Reminder From Michaela,

He is only hot because he is older. There is no other reason. Save yourself some time and mental health problems and date someone your own age!

All my love,

Michaela R.

Other works by Michaela

Between Us, It's Hard

The Soulmate Proposal

The Book Deal: A Novella from The Soulmate Proposal

Milton Keynes UK
Ingram Content Group UK Ltd.
UKHW040037160324
439374UK00005B/332